Sophie and the Scoundrels

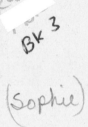

Other books in the growing Faithgirlz!™ library

Best Friends Bible

The Sophie Series

Sophie's World (Book One)
Sophie's Secret (Book Two)
Sophie's Irish Showdown (Book Four)
Sophie's First Dance? (Book Five)
Sophie's Stormy Summer (Book Six)
Sophie Breaks the Code (Book Seven)
Sophie Tracks a Thief (Book Eight)

Nonfiction

No Boys Allowed: Devotions for Girls
Girlz Rock: Devotions for You

Check out www.faithgirlz.com

faiThGirLz!™

Sophie and the Scoundrels

Nancy Rue

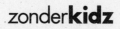

zonder**kidz**

zonderkidz.
The children's group of Zondervan

www.zonderkidz.com

Sophie and the Scoundrels
Copyright © 2005 by Nancy Rue

Requests for information should be addressed to:
Zonderkidz, 5300 Patterson Ave. SE
Grand Rapids, Michigan 49530

Library of Congress Cataloging-in-Publication Data
Rue, Nancy N.

   Sophie and the scoundrels / Nancy Rue.
     p. cm.-(Faithgirlz)
   Summary: Worried that her parents are breaking up, Sophie gets lost in an imaginary world again as she and her friends transform Fiona's tree house into a space station as a school science project, despite sabotage and jealousies.
   ISBN 0-310-70758-7 (softcover)
   [1. Space stations — Fiction. 2. Science projects — Fiction. 3. Family problems — Fiction. 4. Best friends — Fiction. 5. Friendship. 6. Imagination — Fiction. 7. Christian life — Fiction.] I. Title. II. Series.
PZ7.R88515Sj 2005
[Fic]-dc22
                                 2004022918

Published in association with the literary agency of Alive Communications, Inc., 7680 Goddard Street, Suite 200, Colorado Springs, CO 80920.

Photography: Synergy Photographic/Brad Lampe
Illustrations: Grace Chen Design & Illustration
Art direction/design: Michelle Lenger
Interior design: Susan Ambs
Interior composition: Pamela J. L. Eicher

Printed in the United States of America

06 07 08 09 • 8 7 6 5 4

So we fix our eyes not on what is seen, but on what is unseen.
For what is seen is temporary, but what is unseen is eternal.

— 2 Corinthians 4:18

Sunlight hit Sophie LaCroix smack in the eyes as she and her dad stepped

from the NASA building.

Solar rays, Sophie corrected herself. If she was going to make a movie about outer space, she was going to have to start thinking more scientifically.

Her dad grabbed her elbow — just before she stepped off the curb into the employees' parking lot.

"Let me at least get you to the car before you go off into La-La Land," Daddy said.

Sophie gave him her wispy smile. Not because he was right about La-La Land. Her daydreams were much more sophisticated than that. She grinned because he was grinning, instead of scolding her for not paying attention to her surroundings, the way he used to do.

"Sorry," Sophie said. "Did I almost get run over?"

"Not this time," Daddy said. He imitated her high-pitched voice, but that was okay, too. His eyes were doing the good kind of teasing.

Sophie hoisted her pretty-skinny, short self up into Daddy's black Chevrolet pickup that he called the Space Mobile and whipped the light brown strands of her down-to-the-shoulders hair off her face.

I'm going to have to wear it in a braid if I'm going to play an astronaut in the movie, she thought. *You can't have a bunch of hair flying around in your space helmet.*

Did they call them helmets? Would hair actually fly around with that gravity thing they were talking about?

Sophie sighed as she adjusted her glasses. There was so much she was going to have to find out.

"All right, dish, Soph," Daddy said. "Your mind's going about nine hundred miles an hour."

"No, the speed of light — which is faster than anything."

Daddy arched a dark eyebrow over his sunglasses as he passed through the NASA gate. "Somebody was paying attention."

"Okay, so what does NASA stand for again?" Sophie said.

"National Aeronautics and Space Administration."

"Oh." Sophia spun that out in her head. "Then it should be NAASA."

Daddy shook his head. "That would sound like a sheep. NAAAAA."

"What's 'aeronautics'?" She knew she could ask her best friend, Fiona, who knew what every word in life meant, but there was no time to waste. There was a film to be made.

"It's anything that has to do with making and flying aircraft," Daddy said.

Sophie decided she and the Corn Flakes would probably stick to the space part, which had real possibilities.

"Anything else you need to know for your report?" Daddy said.

"My what?"

"Your report. You know — Kids Go to Work with Dads Day. Don't you have to write up something for school?"

"Oh," Sophie said. "Yeah."

Daddy gave her a sideways glance. "Don't think I don't know what's going on in there," he said. He tapped her lightly on the forehead. "You can make your movie. Matter of fact, I WANT you to so you won't leave the planet when you're supposed to be doing your schoolwork."

Sophie nodded. The only reason he had given her the video camera was so she would spin out her dreams on film instead of letting them draw her right out the window when she was in class.

"Can I trust you to do your report as soon as you get home, without my having to check it?"

"No," Sophie said. "You better check it."

Dad chortled. That was the way Fiona always described it when Sophie's dad laughed.

Yeah, Fiona was definitely good with words. Sophie wanted to get her started writing the script right away. And Maggie would need plenty of time to work on costumes. And Kitty had to get the graphics going —

"Earth to Sophie." Daddy landed the truck in the driveway, and Sophie reentered the atmosphere.

"The report. By nineteen hundred hours."

Sophie did a quick calculation in her head. "Seven o'clock," she said.

"Roger," Daddy said.

"Over and out."

Sophie tried to keep a very scientific face on as she ran into the house, headed for the stairs. If she didn't stay completely focused, nineteen hundred hours was going to come and go—and so would the video camera. "Hi, Mama, how are you?" Sophie's mom sarcastically said from the kitchen doorway. "Let me tell you about my day."

Sophie turned around, hand tight on the banister. Mama's brown-like-Sophie's eyes were shining at her, right out of the halo of her curly frosted hair. She looked impish—the way people often said Sophie herself did.

"Hi, Mama," Sophie said. She edged up another step. "I'll tell you all about it later. I have to get my report done."

"Sorry, Mama," Daddy said from behind Sophie's mom. "She has her orders."

Sophie's hand got even tighter on the banister as she watched the happy elf go back inside her mother, to be replaced by a stiff face.

"I see," she said. "You go on then, Dream Girl."

And then Mama turned back to the kitchen without even looking at Daddy.

Sophie hurried up the steps so she wouldn't have to hear the silence that was going to freeze up the whole kitchen. Every time Mama and Daddy were in the same room lately they turned into popsicles. It had been way back before Thanksgiving that she'd last heard them laugh together, and this was January. Sophie closed her bedroom door and headed for her bed with the purple bedspread—the best place for thinking in the whole entire galaxy. As soon as Daddy looked over her paper, she would have the all-clear to dream the dreams that had to come before Corn Flakes Productions—Sophie, Fiona, Kitty, and Maggie—could start on the film.

She sighed happily to herself as she pulled out her notebook, selected the blue-green gel pen—*a very aeronautical color*, she thought—and went to work.

At least it was Mr. Denton, the language arts teacher, she was writing for. He liked it when she wrote about things just the way she saw them. In blue-green words, she took him all the way through the huge telescope where you could see the craters of the moon like they were right next door — and the robotic arm they were building to capture satellites from space shuttles and work on them — and the plants that had actually been grown in space.

She polished it off with the best part: the simulated space station. She'd learned that "simulated" meant it was a fake but it was just like the real thing. She'd been allowed to go into that and see how it orbited all the time and what kind of experiments they did in there in microgravity. She hadn't even heard of that before, and now she could imagine herself there — and that was when it had hit her — what she was supposed to do next.

I know now, Sophie wrote in her final paragraph, *that I am called to make a major film about a brave girl astronaut named —*

Sophie paused, gel pen poised over paper. She didn't quite have the name yet. Daddy would still let it pass without that one detail.

It is my responsibility to put what I have learned on film, she wrote on, *so that others may have their eyes opened —* THAT was brilliant — *to the wonderful world of outer space.*

She signed her name with a flourish and sank back into the pillows to survey her work. There were probably some words spelled wrong, she knew that. She wasn't that good of a student yet — even though she had come a way-long way since she'd started at Great Marsh Elementary back in September. Then she had been failing. That was before she started seeing Dr. Peter. He was her therapist, and he was a Christian like her, and he could help her with ANY problem.

Sophie sat up and cocked an ear toward her door. On the other side of it, she could hear her older sister, Lacie, clamoring up the stairs with her basketball and her gym bag and her backpack full of honors classes books. In the way-far background, her five-year-old brother, Zeke, was watching SpongeBob and yelling out "SquarePants" every couple of minutes.

But other than that, the house was too quiet.

I wonder if Dr. Peter could tell me why Mama and Daddy don't seem to like each other that much anymore, Sophie thought.

But it was a cold thought she couldn't hold without feeling shivers.

Tossing her glasses aside and closing her eyes, Sophie went back to NASA in her mind, back to the space station where the girl astronaut had come into her imagination straight out of the strato-sphere — the absolute highest part of the earth's atmosphere —

Stratosphere! Sophie thought. *That's her — my — last name. No, too long. How about Stratos for short?*

Perfect. After that the first name came easy. Stellar. Like the stars. No, make that Stella.

Stella Stratos. Astronaut Stella Stratos.

Astronaut Stella Stratos looked up from the complicated calcula-tions on her computer screen to see one of her assistants standing in the doorway of the simulator.

"Can't you see I'm working?" Stella said to the clueless young woman.

"No, I can see you're going loopy again."

Sophie blinked. It was Lacie, combing out her wet, curly dark hair and giving Sophie her usual you-are-such-an-airhead look from nar-rowed blue eyes.

"Who are ya today?" Lacie said. Then without waiting for an answer, she said, "Come on; Mama's got dinner ready."

I wonder what they eat when they're traveling in outer space, Sophie thought as she followed Lacie downstairs. There was so much to learn.

Which was why she was ready to get the Corn Flakes right on it the next morning when they met, as always, at the swings before school when it was good weather — and it was perfect for thoughts of filming — a way-rare thing in Virginia in January.

Before they were all even settled into their swings, Sophie was spilling out everything that had happened at NASA. She skimmed the soles of her boots over the slushy puddle that had formed under her swing.

"What's going on?" she said. "Y'all are looking at me weird."

"It isn't weirdness," Fiona said. "It's envy."

She cocked her head at Sophie so that one panel of golden-brown hair fell over a gray eye. Her usually creamy-coffee skin was chappy-red with the cold.

"Envy?" Sophie said. That was a stretch, seeing how Fiona was way rich and had more stuff even than the Corn Pops did. Those were the popular girls who practically wore their clothes inside out so everybody could see their labels.

Fiona tightened the hood on her North Face jacket. "I had the most boring day in life yesterday. I couldn't go to work with my dad, so I went with my mom."

"But your mom's a doctor," Kitty said. Her blue eyes were wider than they were most of the time. Everything surprised Kitty. She really was like a cat.

Fiona twitched her eyebrows. "That means she sees patients all day long — and that means I had to sit in the office with her receptionist and see her like once every twenty minutes. At lunchtime, I called my Boppa to come pick me up."

"Yeah," Maggie said. "That's boring." She spoke in her thud-voice, so that every word came out like the final say on just about anything. Sophie sometimes wondered if that was because Maggie was Cuban, and English wasn't her native language. Fiona always said it was just because Maggie was bossy.

"Mine was even boringer than yours," Kitty said. She was starting to whine, and she flipped her ponytail. She did both of those things a lot. "I didn't get to spend that much time with my dad, either, since he's a pilot."

"You didn't get to go up in a plane?" Sophie said.

"She couldn't," Maggie said. "It's the Air Force. They don't let civilians fly in their planes."

"How do YOU know, Maggie?" Fiona said.

It's only 8:15 in the morning, Sophie thought, *and they're already getting on each other's nerves.*

"What about you, Maggie?" Sophie said.

Maggie shrugged. "I don't have a dad. I went to work with my mom, but that was no big deal because I go to work with her every Saturday."

"But she does such cool stuff!" Sophie said. Maggie's mother was a tailor, and she made all the costumes for their films. Sophie thought Senora LaQuita was the most talented Cuban woman she'd ever met. Actually, she was the only Cuban woman she'd ever met.

"So you see why we have father-envy, Soph," Fiona was saying. "You had the best day of any of us."

"I bet I know what you're going to say, Sophie," Maggie said.

"No, you don't, Maggie," Fiona said. "Nobody knows what somebody else is thinking."

"She's going to say she wants to make a movie about astronauts," Maggie said.

Sophie looked at Fiona. "That WAS what I was going to say."

The bell rang, telling them they only had five minutes to get to first period. "You don't get to say anything now," Maggie said. "We have to go."

"She KNOWS that," Fiona said.

But she didn't get to say anything else, either, because as Sophie gave one more swing before she got out — the earth seemed to give way under her.

Actually, it was the seat of the swing, and before Sophie could even imagine herself falling through space, she was sitting — hard — in the ice-slushy puddle.

2

hands down and haul her up. She could feel the cold muckiness on the seat of her brand-new jeans. It wasn't hard to picture the embroidered flowers on the pockets with mud caked between their petals.

"Oh, man!" she wailed. "This feels disgusting!"

"Are you okay?" Kitty said. She was whining louder than Sophie.

"I just feel gross!"

"It isn't that bad," Fiona said — without even looking at the back of Sophie's jeans.

Maggie did. She looked soberly at Sophie and said, "Yes, it is. You've got mud all the way down to your ankles. It even got on your coat."

"Enough already!" Fiona said. She glared at Maggie as she peeled off her jacket. "Tie this around your waist and nobody will even notice 'til we get to the office."

"Yes, they will," Maggie said. "She's dripping on the ground."

"That's gonna leave a trail," Kitty put in.

"Would you two cease and desist?" Fiona said. Sophie knew she meant "Shut up!"

"Just walk tall and stare straight ahead," Fiona whispered to Sophie as she guided her through the doors into the school.

"This is so embarrassing," Sophie whispered back.

"Not if nobody even looks at you."

Fat chance. Of course the first people they saw were Anne-Stuart, Willoughby, B.J., and Queen Bee Julia — the Corn Pops. They were popular — which was why the Corn Flakes called them Pops — and as far as the CFs were concerned, they were pretty corny as well. When the Corn Pops had once referred to Sophie and her friends as "flakes," they adopted the name proudly. At least it made them different from THOSE girls.

THOSE girls were currently staring with their hands over their lip-glossy mouths. They didn't say anything, because they'd gotten in enough trouble for bullying the Corn Flakes before Christmas to keep them watching their backs until they went to college. Even Ms. Quelling, the social studies teacher who thought they were perfect, kept her eye on them.

As Sophie squished toward the office, Willoughby Wiley, as usual, giggled out of control in a voice so shrill it set Sophie's nose hairs on end. Julia Cummings, who stood a head taller than all of them like an imperious monarch (Fiona's words), had her eyes slit downward in scorn for her subjects.

At her side was her handmaiden, B.J. Freeman, whose eternally red cheeks appeared to be on fire with the sheer triumph of seeing Sophie humiliated.

The only one even pretending to show sympathy was Anne-Stuart Riggins. But that was the way with Anne-Stuart, Sophie reminded herself as she sloshed past. She snorted in Sophie's direction, her powder-blue eyes watering with what was either held-back laughter or some pretty hideous allergies. Sophie wished she would sneeze her brains out right now.

"Why did THEY have to be here?" Sophie muttered to Fiona as they passed.

"They're always where you don't want them to be," Fiona muttered back. "Ignore them. They're so not worth it."

But it was almost impossible to ignore a knot of sixth-grade boys who stood just beyond the office door like they were holding up the wall. They were all wearing baggy jeans big enough for Sophie's entire family. And T-shirts down to their knees, and high-tech tennis shoes and short haircuts that outlined the shapes of their heads — the only thing that was different among them.

Eddie Wornom, Sophie knew, was the one with the big ol' square head over his bruiser of a body. He was clapping like an ape. Sophie expected a swearword to slip out of his mouth any minute, which always happened when he was excited.

The one with the long head was Colton Messik. His ears stuck out like open car doors, and he was always pretending he was shooting a basketball. Right now he was too hysterical for that.

And then there was the third kid. Tod Ravelli. He was like a male version of Julia, except he was short and had a head that came to a point in the front like he was from Whoville. Sophie always thought he could have been a model for one of Dr. Seuss's books.

But there was nothing funny about him in Sophie's world. He was looking at her now like she had dared crawl across his path in her state of degradation (Fiona again). "Who dragged you in?" he said.

"I did," Fiona said. "You got a problem with that?"

"Yeah," Eddie chimed in. "I smell something. Ooh — she pooped her pants!"

"No she didn't, stupid," Maggie said. "That's mud."

Eddie and Colton looked at each other and sniffed.

"No," Colton said. "That's poop."

Then they collapsed into each other, while Tod continued to stare at Sophie as if he could make her disappear.

She wished she would.

Fiona was about to shove Sophie into the office when Tod said, "Dude, just don't get any of that on me."

Fiona looked at Sophie with a familiar gleam in her eyes — a gleam Sophie could read.

"One," Sophie whispered to her.

"Two," Fiona whispered back.

"Three!" they said together.

And then Fiona whipped the jacket from around Sophie's waist and stepped back — and Sophie shook like a wet dog.

Big drops of mud, slush, and general playground filth flew off Sophie and into the air like dirty confetti. Most of it landed on Tod, speckling him in drooly brown. What didn't get on him found its resting place on Colton and Eddie. Somewhere between "One" and "Two," Maggie and Kitty had known enough to dive behind a trash can.

Shouts of "Man!" "Dude!" and "Sick!" came out of the now mud-caked trio, along with a few words from Eddie that Sophie knew she wouldn't be repeating when she told this story to Mama. While the boys were frantically de-grossing, Fiona, Sophie, Maggie, and Kitty dived into the office and shut the door behind them.

"Score," Fiona whispered.

Even Maggie agreed.

While the school secretary called Sophie's mom to bring dry clothes, Maggie gave Sophie another once-over.

"I can tell you how to get those stains out," she said.

"Just don't share that information with that bunch of Fruit Loops," Fiona said.

Kitty giggled. "Fruit Loops!"

"That's what they are." Fiona wiggled her eyebrows. "But they're SO obvious. We can handle them."

When they left the office, Sophie could hear Kitty whining all the way down the hall, "What if I don't WANT to 'handle them'?"

Sophie couldn't wait to describe the whole thing to Mama when she got there. Mama was sure to love this little tale.

But when Mama arrived, Sophie felt the story shrivel up on her lips. Mama's eyes were red and puffy—like she'd been crying. And not the sweet way Mama had of bawling over the lopsided craft projects Sophie and Lacie and Zeke had brought home to her over the years. This looked like serious crying that Mama was trying to hide under makeup she hardly ever wore.

"What's wrong, Mama?" Sophie said.

Mama gave a watery smile as she handed over a whole different outfit, down to Sophie's favorite toe socks with the frogs on them.

"I think I'm just coming down with a cold," she said.

But Sophie had seen watery-eyed colds on Anne-Stuart. This was a whole other thing.

"Do you need a hug?" Sophie said.

Mama enfolded her in her arms, shuddered a little, and then pulled away and headed straight for the door, waving over her shoulder. But Sophie had seen the tears already splashing onto her cheeks.

Sophie had a blur over her own eyes as she sat on the bathroom floor and fed her toes into the socks. *This doesn't feel good at all. What could possibly be this wrong?*

She couldn't shake it off the way she'd gotten rid of the mud. As she wriggled into fresh jeans, she thought about Dr. Peter. She only got to talk to him alone every other week now.

Next week I'm going to ask him what to do, she thought.

Only — next week was a whole long way away. The chill that shivered her insides could freeze her solid in seven days. In three days. Maybe in one.

Astronaut Stella Stratos pulled the regulation NASA turtleneck sweater over her head and straightened her shoulders. This was serious family business, but she couldn't let it distract her from the work at hand. There was a movie to be made about a creation that could save the world. Somehow. She had not yet figured that part out.

Sophie knew that if she kept her mind on Stella, she'd find the way to rescue the planet. AND keep the cold thought of Mama crying away in some dark place, where it couldn't hurt so much.

The Fruit Loops spent the rest of the day making disgusting

3

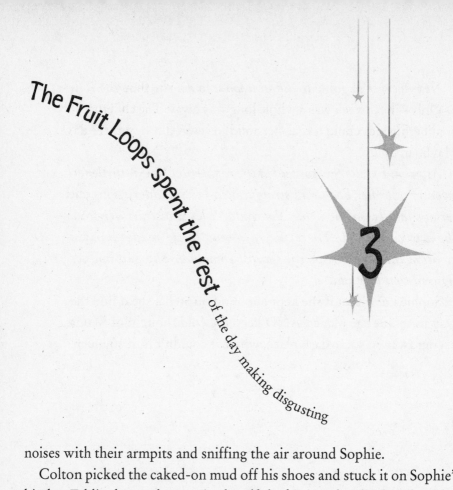

noises with their armpits and sniffing the air around Sophie.

Colton picked the caked-on mud off his shoes and stuck it on Sophie's binder. Eddie dumped an entire handful of it into her backpack and during lunch, all three of them made such a big deal out of telling people to watch out because she had run out of Pampers, Sophie stuffed her peanut butter and jelly sandwich back into her lunch box with only one bite taken out of it.

"Don't let them get to you," Fiona said. "They're just imbeciles."

"What's an 'imbecile'?" Kitty said.

"Idiot," Maggie told her. "Them."

She nodded toward the three boys, two of whom were pulling a chair out from under Eddie and making a splatting noise with their very big mouths when he hit the floor.

"That's you falling out of the swing," Maggie said to Sophie.

"Duh," Fiona said.

"I'm just wondering how they knew the swing broke under me." Sophie blinked at the Corn Flakes. "We were the only ones left on the playground when it happened."

"I know how."

Sophie looked down the cafeteria table at Harley Hunter. She was an into-every-sport girl, only as far as Sophie was concerned she wasn't stuck-up like Lacie. She and her friends Gill, Nikki, and Vette — the Wheaties — sat at the Corn Flakes' lunch table most days and never made fun of them.

"How?" Kitty said to Harley.

"Because we heard those boys talking at P.E. yesterday."

"They had it planned," Gill said. "They were going to do something to the swing because they knew y'all sit there every morning."

"Hello!" Fiona said. Her gray eyes were practically popping out. "Why didn't you tell us?"

"They're morons," Harley said.

"Imbeciles," Kitty said.

"Whatever. The way they were laughing about it, we thought they were just messing around."

"We didn't think they had enough brains to know how to set up a swing to break," Gill said.

Maggie scraped back her chair. "I'm telling."

"NO!" said all the Wheaties.

Kitty's whine echoed them.

"You're probably right," Fiona said. "You tell on them, and the next thing you know, all of you are in a mud puddle. Or worse."

Maggie was looking hard at Sophie, who squirmed in her seat.

"Okay," Sophie said. "But we can't let them get away with bullying. We made a pact."

"What's a 'pact' again?" Kitty said.

Sometimes it seemed like Kitty must have failed all her vocabulary tests since second grade.

"It was our promise that we made," Sophie said patiently. "We can't let mean people get away with stuff just because we're afraid of them."

"But I can't afford to get in trouble," Harley said. "Or I won't be allowed to play basketball."

"I still think I should tell," Maggie said

Fiona was giving Sophie the best friend's I'll-do-whatever-you-think-we-oughta-do look.

"Don't tell yet," Sophie said to Maggie. "Like Fiona said before, I bet we can handle those imbeciles ourselves."

Gill put up a hand. It took Sophie a good five seconds to realize Gill wanted to high-five.

"You're tough," Gill said to her. "I dig that."

Actually, sitting in the middle of seven girls who were all way bigger than she was, Sophie had never felt more wimpy in her life. But she closed her eyes and imagined Jesus — just the way Dr. Peter had taught her to.

As usual, she didn't imagine Jesus saying anything. Dr. Peter said that would be like making up God. But it felt good to know he was just a thought away.

Help me to do the no-bully thing, please, she asked him. *Please don't let me be the wimp the Fruit Loops think I am.*

Something else made her wonder, though, as she suffered through PE with the Fruit Loops splashing in every puddle within three feet of her, and through math class where they delivered fake dry-cleaning bills to her desk.

Why, she thought, *are the Fruit Loops all of a sudden trying to get to me? I never did anything to them. I never even hardly noticed them that much until yesterday.*

I don't even LIKE boys.

As she tried to settle into last-period science class, Sophie went back to the promise she'd made — the Flakes would "handle" the Fruit Loops.

"How we will do that," Astronaut Stella said to her crew, *"I have not yet determined. But never fear. Science will be victorious."*

Sophie was still enjoying the view from the space capsule when Fiona coughed at her. That was the signal that Sophie was about to miss something important in class. Like an assignment.

Sophie focused on Mrs. Utley, whose many chins were wobbling as she passed out blue sheets of paper to the class with her pretty, plump hands. The Corn Pops called her Mrs. Fatley behind her back, but Sophie thought there was just more of her to be beautiful than most people.

"This will explain what I want in your science project," Mrs. Utley was saying. As she passed Colton's desk, he gave her a teacher's pet grin, and then behind her back blew up his cheeks with air at Eddie, who nearly fell out of his desk.

Like he has room to laugh at her, Sophie thought. *Pig Boy.*

"I'd like for you to work in groups," Mrs. Utley went on.

The Corn Flakes all looked at one another. The Wheaties high-fived one other, and every Corn Pop grabbed onto another Corn Pop's arm like Mrs. Utley was going to dare to try pry them apart.

Tod just gave the other Fruit Loops a nod like their working together was a done deal.

"Let's cut a frog up!" Eddie said.

"Sick, man," Colton said back.

"Yeah — that's what I'm sayin'."

"Dude, I'll puke."

"Wimp."

"Loser."

"MAJOR loser."

"I have a scathingly brilliant idea!" Fiona said to the Corn Flakes.

"Is 'scathingly' a good thing?" Kitty said.

"It is when it tells us what to do for our project." Fiona grinned at Sophie, wiggling her eyebrows at light speed. "Actually, you told us. You're the one who went to NASA. You're the one whose father is a rocket scientist. It only makes sense — we build a space station." She gave the eyebrows a final wiggle. "And I know the perfect place to do it."

"Where?" Maggie said.

"My place. Tree house. I'm the only one in the family that's allowed to go up in it. Except Boppa, of course."

Sophie loved the image of Fiona's amazing grandfather up in the tree house, bald head gleaming in the sun, hammering away at anything Fiona asked him to.

"Not only will we build a space station — " Sophie said.

"Let me guess," Maggie said. "We'll film the whole thing and have costumes and play like we're astronauts."

"Do you have a problem with that?" Fiona said to her.

Maggie shook her head. Kitty was dimpling all over.

"I'll need your plan by Wednesday," Mrs. Utley was saying. "And those of you who are in the GATE program, keep in mind that you will need to do more of the work than the other people in your groups."

For once, that wasn't a problem for Sophie. She had just gotten into the Gifted and Talented Education program — with Fiona —

right before Christmas, and so far she'd felt like somebody had made a mistake putting her there. But this? This was her life every day.

Fiona whipped open the purple Treasures Book that she always carried around for the Corn Flakes, and Maggie handed her a fresh pencil with a very sharp point and a no-mistakes-yet eraser. "Start dictating, Soph," she said.

Sophie sighed happily and let Astronaut Stella Stratos take her rightful place at the podium. The plan to save the planet began.

Sophie would have asked Mama's permission to go over to Fiona's the

next day the minute she got home from school, but Mama was dealing with Lacie, who was having a boy crisis. Sophie was more sure than ever that males weren't worth the time it took to learn their names.

After that it was kind of funky at the dinner table. Lacie was brooding over Mr. Boy and picking at her pot roast. Mama and Daddy were talking like the people on the news — all polite with stiff laughter at things that weren't that funny. And Zeke dumped his milk over, crawled under the table three times to get his napkin, and once nibbled at Lacie's calf while he was under there.

Right after dinner, Mama left for a meeting at church, and Sophie paced her bedroom floor, the way she was sure

Astronaut Stella would do when she was faced with a delay on a project. Fiona was probably that very minute searching the Internet, while Maggie and her mother were drawing pictures of costumes and Kitty was thinking of an astronaut name for herself. Sophie had learned that she had to give Kitty plenty of time to come up with these things. Her imagination muscle was still a little weak.

Mama wasn't home at bedtime, so Sophie padded out of her room in her pajamas-with-the-feet-in-them to go ask Daddy for permission. Lacie was coming back from the phone with wet eyelashes when Sophie passed her in the upstairs hall.

"Why are you wearing those?" Lacie said, pointing to Sophie's floppy feet. "You look like you're two years old."

Sophie didn't point out that it was the closest thing she had to a space suit right now. She'd learned not to share that kind of information with Lacie. Instead, she said, "Have you been crying?"

"Yes," Lacie said. Her voice got thick. "Take a little advice from me, Soph. Don't ever get a crush on a guy who turns out to be a two-faced, coldhearted little — "

"Imbecile," Sophie said.

Lacie's eyebrows shot up. "Yeah. That's the perfect word."

Sophie took a deep breath. "Mama's been crying a lot lately, too," she said. "Do you think she thinks Daddy is a two-timing, coldhearted little imbecile? Well, big imbecile."

"No, I do NOT!" Lacie said. "She and Daddy are good together!"

"Oh," Sophie said. "Then how come they hardly talk to each other anymore?"

"They DO." Lacie set her face so firmly, even her freckles seemed to stand at attention. "You just don't hear them."

"Do you hear them?" Sophie said.

"No. I don't go spying on them."

"Then how do you know?"

Sophie knew she was starting to sound like Maggie, but she couldn't stop herself.

Lacie gave her an annoyed look. "I just know," she said.

Rolling her arms up into one of Daddy's old T-shirts she was wearing, Lacie flounced to her room.

She's scared, too, Sophie thought. *That scares ME.*

But Daddy himself didn't seem scared when Sophie found him, bending his big handsome head toward his computer screen, cup of coffee at his side. Sophie knew it was decaf. He and Mama usually had their mugs of it together at night.

"What's up, Soph?" he said. He glanced at her and drew his eyebrows in over his nose. "Nice outfit. I wish your mother had a pair of those. She has the coldest feet when she goes to bed, and she puts them right on *me.*"

Mama and Daddy touching feet was good, Sophie decided. Although, she couldn't imagine touching some guy's feet. The image of Eddie Wornom coming after her with his huge clodhoppers made her nauseous.

"You okay?" Daddy said.

"Yes, sir. I just wanted to ask Mama if I could go to Fiona's after school tomorrow."

Daddy took a slurp of his coffee and squinted his eyes like it was hot. Sophie could never figure out why grown-ups couldn't just wait until it cooled off a little bit.

"I don't see why not," he said. "I'll tell your mom."

"When's she coming home?"

He stopped in mid-gulp. "I can speak for her," he said. "It's fine."

There was something pointy in his voice, like she'd just told him he wasn't the boss of her.

She got on tiptoes to kiss his cheek. "I was just asking," she said. "Lacie's crying again."

Daddy's eyes suddenly got round. "The boy thing?" he said.

Sophie nodded.

"Now THAT I'll leave for Mama to handle."

On her way up the stairs Sophie wondered why Daddy couldn't explain boys to Lacie. After all, he was a boy once.

It was sunny again the next day and not even cold enough for gloves. That meant it would be even warmer when she and the Corn Flakes climbed up into the tree house that afternoon. Sophie was almost too excited to eat her Cream of Wheat, and she considered feeding it to Zeke, who was crawling around under the snack bar.

"Did Daddy tell you I'm going to Fiona's after school?" she said.

Mama's hand tightened on the knife she was using to spread peanut butter. "Yes, he did. I wish you had talked to me first. I have an appointment with Dr. Peter today and I was counting on you watching Zeke for me in the waiting room."

The Cream of Wheat turned into a lump in Sophie's throat. "You mean, I can't go to Fiona's?"

Mama put a top on the sandwich like she was slamming a door. "Maybe I can get Boppa to watch Zeke over there. I just don't like to take advantage of him."

"He won't mind!" Sophie said.

Mama dropped the sandwich into Sophie's lunch box and snapped it just a little too hard. "I said I'll ask him. Zeke, PLEASE get up in your chair. I don't have time for this today."

It seemed to Sophie that Mama had as much time as she always did in the morning. She told herself Mama must have gotten home late and she was cranky because she didn't get enough sleep. Now Sophie was a little cranky herself. If she didn't get to go to Fiona's, their group was going to start off their project already behind.

"Boppa will watch Zeke — you know he will," Fiona said when Sophie told her the news later on the playground.

The Corn Flakes were all gathered at the end of the slide. Even though somebody had fixed the swing, they weren't taking any chances.

"He's better behaved than our two brats," Fiona said.

Sophie had to nod. Fiona's four-year-old sister, Isabella, and her six-year-old brother, Rory, went through a new nanny about every three months. The last one, Marissa, had left after Rory sneaked miniature LEGOs into her quesadilla and she broke a tooth.

"If you can't come," Maggie said to Sophie, "we'll just have to start without you."

"We will NOT start without our captain." Fiona saluted Sophie.

"How come she's the captain?" Maggie said.

"I like it when Sophie's captain," Kitty said. "She's nice."

"And she has the camera, and the resources," Fiona said. "It's most advantageous for us to make her captain."

"What's 'advantageous'?" all three of them said.

Fiona looked straight at Maggie. "It means it doesn't make sense for us to do it any other way. Besides, Boppa will take care of Z-Boy and Sophie will be there and we'll go on like we planned."

"I'm bringing Tang for us to drink," Kitty said. "My father told me they drink that in outer space."

Sophie was impressed.

Mama did pick Sophie up that afternoon with Zeke in the car and dropped them both off at Fiona's.

"Don't worry, Lynda," Boppa said to Sophie's Mom as Zeke bolted across Fiona's yard toward Isabella and Rory. "I won't let them hurt him."

He smiled at Mama, but his dark caterpillar eyebrows drooped, and his forehead wrinkled halfway up his shiny head. It didn't make Sophie feel any better that Boppa seemed worried about Mama, too.

By the time Fiona came out to meet Sophie, flanked by Kitty and Maggie, Rory and Isabella were already screaming and chasing Zeke in and out of the line of cedar trees that bordered Fiona's huge lawn, which actually had water splashing deliciously over a stone wall and a little bridge that crossed the pond the waterfall made. So many filming possibilities—

But today Sophie was much more interested in the tree house.

It was built off three big pine trees so that it was a triangle, and the only way to get to it was on a ladder that went absolutely straight up through a narrow opening in the tree-house floor. Even tiny Sophie had to scrunch her shoulders together to slide through.

As the Corn Flakes climbed, a lady stood at the bottom, tucking a big jar of a very orange-looking liquid, some plastic cups, and individual bags of pretzels into a basket that was attached to a rope on a crank handle. Sophie knew that was for transporting stuff up to the tree house. She'd been up there several times before—just not for business this important.

Sophie leaned over the railing to watch her. The lady had perfectly curled hair down to her shoulders and teeth as white as Tic-Tacs.

"Is she part of our ground crew?" Sophie whispered to Fiona.

"She can be," Fiona said. "Actually, she's the new nanny. Her name's Kateesha."

"She doesn't look like she has any bruises yet," Maggie said.

Kitty stroked dreamily at her own hair. "She looks like Halle Berry. I wish I looked like that."

Maggie shook her head. "You'll never look like that. You're Caucasian."

"But you're just as pretty," Sophie put in quickly. It wouldn't be good to start off with Kitty in tears.

Boppa had built lockers against the railings that had lids on hinges so the girls could put stuff in them, and Sophie put her backpack in hers. She was already pretending it was a spaceship compartment. The basket arrived through the ladder hole and Fiona said, "We should eat first. We're going to need sustenance if we want our minds to be sharp."

"Define 'sustenance,'" Kitty said.

"Food," Maggie told her. "I don't know why she couldn't just say that."

"Because 'sustenance' sounds more scientific," Fiona said.

Sophie was already pouring the orange stuff into cups. A few grainy things floated to the top of each one.

"What is it?" Maggie said as she stared into hers.

"It's the Tang I was telling you about," Kitty said proudly. "It comes in this powder stuff and you mix it with water."

"Somebody didn't mix it up enough," Maggie said.

Fiona drained hers and pulled the Treasures Book out from under her arm. "Captain," she said to Sophie, "do I have your permission to present information?"

"Yes," Sophie said. "But please call me Stella. Stella Stratos."

"I haven't thought of a name yet," Kitty said. Her voice was starting to wind up.

"That can wait," Fiona said.

"I thought Sophie was captain," Maggie said.

Sophie pointed at the book. "Let's see your information."

It would be advantageous for us to get this going, Stella thought, *or I'm going to have a mutiny on my hands.*

Fiona produced some pages that she had printed off the Internet. Like about twenty. Fiona never did anything halfway.

"Your report please, Crew Member," Sophie said to her.

Fiona cleared her throat, very scientifically, Sophie thought — and pointed to a paragraph. "We would actually be called an expedition crew. We're building an international space station that will weigh a million pounds when it's done and there'll be six laboratories in it for research."

"Do the stations have names?" Sophie said.

Fiona frowned importantly over the page. "One's Destiny. They call one Leonardo."

Kitty squealed. "Let's call ours that!"

"We're going to need to get to know the station before we name it," Sophie said.

"Like a puppy?" Maggie said.

"Is this a picture of it?" Sophie pointed to a long narrow shiny vehicle that had two enormous flat wings above it and so many robot-like arms she expected it to come alive right on the page. Her heart actually started to race. Yeah, this had more dreaming tucked into it than anything she had ever thought up before.

"We're gonna build that?" Maggie said. She pulled her chin back into her neck.

"Something like it," Sophie said.

"That's so cool," Kitty said. "I want to work this thing." She poked a finger at the robotic arm that hung down like a big metal sea serpent.

"What does it do?" Maggie said.

"I don't know," Kitty said. "I just think it's cute."

"Science can't be cute," Fiona said. "It can be fascinating, and it can be exciting, and it can be scintillating — "

"I'll go with exciting," Kitty said.

Sophie crawled over to her box again. "I'm gonna get the camera and take some before pictures."

"We should think of what we're trying to prove for our project," Maggie said. "I mean ..." She wagged her head a little.

"Shouldn't we, Captain? Mrs. Utley said we have to put that in our plan, and it's due tomorrow."

"That's true," Fiona said. She looked to Sophie like she would rather have admitted she had rabies than agree with Maggie.

"I trust you all to do that while I film," Sophie said.

Fiona, Kitty, and Maggie bent their heads over Fiona's pages, and she explained the basics of what a space station did. Sophie filmed the storage boxes and the railing and the hole for the ladder that had its own hinged door that had to be kept closed when they were up there so that nobody would accidentally fall through — Boppa's rule.

As she captured the tree house with her camera, Sophie had to admit that it was pretty cool just as it was. It was like being on top of the planet, above even the grown-up world.

I want to just lie on my back and look up, Sophie thought. She imagined closing her eyes and dreaming up Captain Stella Stratos for hours on end.

"Are you filming with your eyes closed?" Maggie said.

Sophie popped her eyes open. Oh, yeah. The before movie. No matter how much she loved this tree house as it was, it was soon going to be transformed.

"We have agreed on an experiment, Captain," Fiona said.

"We didn't vote on it," Maggie said.

"So we'll vote already," Fiona said between clenched teeth. "Who wants to make building the space station the experiment, and we tell how it's different from building it in outer space?"

She, Kitty, and Maggie all raised their hands.

"Why did we just do that?" Fiona said.

Sophie gave a hurried nod. "Then it's decided. Now I want to film each of you stating your name and what your job is."

Of course, Sophie had to immediately turn off the camera and help everybody figure out a name and a job, and make sure Fiona didn't get sick of Maggie and haul off and smack her. If that happened, there would be more screaming than they were hearing from down below. It sounded like somebody had somebody tied up. Sophie was afraid to look. She hoped it wasn't that pretty Kateesha lady.

It was decided that Sophie definitely would be Captain Stella Stratos, the head of the space station. Maggie pointed out that Fiona actually knew more about space stations than Sophie did, but Kitty and Fiona overruled her.

Fiona was to be called Jupiter. She was in charge of the experiment itself. Maggie couldn't argue with that, since she'd already said Fiona was better for the job. Besides, Fiona needed to do more because of GATE.

The name they gave Kitty was Luna, after the moon. She kept repeating it like she was afraid she would forget it. Fiona said Kitty should be her assistant.

By the time they got to Maggie, she had picked out her own name: Nimbus. She told them it was a type of cloud.

"I know," Fiona said. "A very DARK cloud."

Kitty nodded. "She does have black hair. I wish I had hair like yours, Maggie."

Maggie looked all around the tree house like she didn't know where to put a compliment.

"I think I should keep all the records of the results of the experiment," Maggie said finally. "I'm the only one of us who's really good at that."

"Hello! Rude!" Fiona said.

"Who always gets hundreds in spelling and handwriting?"

"I get 97's."

"So I'm better at it than you."

"You're the record keeper, Nimbus," Sophie said. She was suddenly so tired, she wanted to crawl into her wooden box. Or maybe put Maggie in hers.

Captain Stella Stratos knew she was going to have to figure out how to handle crew members who always acted like they wanted to throw each other into the ozone layer.

Just then the loudest scream yet pierced the air from the ground right up to the space station. The Corn Flakes all scrambled to the railing, just in time to see Zeke flying off the deck, frantically flapping his little arms, which were clad in a pair of flowered pillowcases. As Sophie watched in horror, her little brother hit the ground like a crashing plane, pillowcases crumpled on either side.

And then he just stayed there, and he didn't move at all.

By the time Sophie got to Zeke, Boppa and Kateesha were already there. Isabella

5

and Rory were nowhere in sight.

"Is he dead?" Sophie said. She slid in on her knees and peered, terrified, at Zeke.

"No, he's not dead," Kateesha said. "But I know two other kids who are going to be when I get a hold of them."

"You go take care of them," Boppa said to her. "Just try not to break any bones."

Kateesha hurried off, and Zeke started to cry. That definitely meant he wasn't dead.

"Where do you hurt, little buddy?" Boppa said.

"Everywhere!" Zeke wailed.

"Is his whole body broken?" Sophie said. "Should we call 911?"

"Let's take a look here," Boppa said. His voice was as soft and calm as always.

He went over Zeke limb by limb. Everything seemed to be in working order. The ice-cream sandwich Kateesha brought him and the apologies from Isabella and Rory got him smiling again. Personally, Sophie didn't think he should forgive those two little monsters. They didn't seem all that sincere to her.

"Why did you jump off the deck in the first place?" Mama asked Zeke later on the way home.

"I didn't jump," Zeke said. "Izzy and Rory pushed me."

"Why did they push you?"

"They wanted to see if I could fly with those wings we made."

Mama glanced at him in the rearview mirror. "Let me tell you something, Z," she said. "You cannot fly. Period. So don't try it again."

"Sophie and them's gonna fly," he said. His bee sting of a mouth was going into a pout.

"No, we're not!" Sophie said. "We're just building a space station."

Mama lowered her voice and leaned a little toward Sophie. "Just to be on the safe side, don't ever take him up into that tree house."

Sophie gave her a somber nod. And then she let out a long breath of relieved air. At least Mama didn't say Sophie couldn't go over to Fiona's and take Zeke from then on. From the serious way she'd seen Mama talking to Boppa before they started for home, Sophie suspected Mama was going to have more sessions with Dr. Peter.

For the next week, the astronauts worked every minute they had setting up the space station. They decided to call it *Freedom 4*. "Freedom" because it was going to save the world, although Captain Stella Stratos hadn't yet figured out how that was going to work. And "Four" sounded the best with "Freedom." When they got to the space station the day after they named it, there was a painted sign up there that read, "Welcome to *Freedom 4*," and all the names on the boxes had been switched to the girls' astronaut names.

Boppa was doing a lot to help them, but they were being very careful to do most of the work themselves with Boppa just overseeing. Mrs. Utley said nobody was allowed to have their parents do their science projects for them.

"These are going to go on display in the science fair for the PTO meeting next month," she told the class. Her chins were really wiggling, so Sophie knew she meant business. "But if any group turns in a project that was obviously done by an adult, it will not be shown. Period."

Sophie heard the Corn Pops whispering to one another like startled bees. As for the Fruit Loops — they were all leaning back in their chairs with their arms folded over their chests. *They think they could get away with having a brain surgeon do their whole project,* Sophie thought. She wondered how many poor frogs they had tortured already.

"How are we going to get all this into the cafeteria to put on display?" Maggie said that afternoon when they were up in the space station.

Sophie looked around at all they'd done so far — the "robot arm" they'd made from an umbrella handle and attached to the basket crank so they could move it up and down; the sets of old headphones from Kitty's dad on hooks for the astronauts; the big flat wings that hung above them that Boppa had helped them make from sheets of metal off a torn-down shed. Captain Stella had to admit that Nimbus had a point.

"Simple," Fiona said. "We'll get Mrs. Utley to set up a DVD player and a TV to show our film, and we'll find some really cool way to display our results. You know, a graph or something. That's your job, Nimbus."

Maggie frowned. "But I need information about that microgravity thing where everything floats around up in space, so I'll know how this is different. That's your job, Jupiter." Maggie's voice then gave its final thud — "Are you two doing any work at all?"

She pointed a stern finger at Kitty and Fiona. Kitty shrank back like she'd been hit with a large stick. Fiona's nostrils flared.

Uh-oh, Sophie thought. *Here it comes.*

"And what about you?" Fiona said. "I don't see any costumes yet. Hello!"

It wasn't the first time Fiona had gotten furious with Maggie since they'd started working on the space station. And Sophie really couldn't blame her. Maggie was getting bossier by the second, and even though sometimes she was right, Kitty whined to Sophie privately that she didn't have to be so mean about it.

"I got enough of that when I was a Corn Pop," she told Sophie. "I thought being a Corn Flake meant you were nice to people."

When Maggie wasn't around, Jupiter was all for voting her off the crew, but Sophie said no. For one thing, how was Maggie supposed to get a science project done if they kicked her out of the group? Mrs. Utley's chins would wiggle right off her face.

"Besides," Sophie told Fiona the next morning at school before Maggie got there, "we're Corn Flakes. We're supposed to help people."

"We're supposed to keep them from being bullied," Fiona said. "I feel like Nimbus is bullying us."

Sophie had noticed that Fiona always referred to Maggie as Nimbus now. She seemed to like the way she could curl her upper lip when she said it. Maggie definitely wasn't bringing out the best in Fiona.

"I'll talk to her," Sophie said. "That's my job as captain."

"Good," Fiona said. "Here she comes. You can start right now."

Fiona tested a swing and then sat down on it, arms folded. Sophie moved away from her a little and stopped Maggie before she could get too close.

"Hi, Mags," Sophie said.

"You should make up your mind what you want to call me," Maggie said. "Sometimes I'm Nimbus. Sometimes I'm Maggie. Now I'm Mags."

"Giving somebody nicknames means you like them," Sophie said.

"Oh," Maggie said. "My mother just calls me Margarita."

Sophie felt her eyes getting big. "Your real name is Margarita?"

"Yes, like the drink. And don't tell anybody at this school, or I'll be laughed at every minute."

Sophie made an X mark on her chest with her hand. "I would never do that. No Corn Flake would ever do that."

"You guys are always nice," Maggie said.

"You're a Corn Flake, too, remember." Sophie sucked in some air. "And, Mags, sometimes you aren't all that nice to certain people in the group."

Maggie's eyes darted in Fiona's direction. "Did SHE tell you that?"

"She didn't have to," Sophie said. "I can see it for myself."

"She isn't the nicest person in the whole world, either." Maggie's words were now firing out like bullets.

"What does THAT mean?" Fiona said. The swing was swaying crazily where she'd lurched out of it.

"It means you've been talking trash about me to Sophie," Maggie said.

Fiona stopped just inches from Maggie's face. Sophie tried to wedge her way between them.

"I never said anything to Sophie that wasn't true," she said.

Fiona's nostrils were flaring so wide, Sophie figured Mama could drive their old Suburban through one of them.

"Why didn't you just say it to me?" Maggie said.

"Okay," Fiona said. "I'll say it straight to your face!"

"Say it, then," Maggie said.

"Okay." Fiona narrowed her eyes at Maggie. "I think you are the bossiest person on the face of the earth. You act like you're the president of the United States or somebody! Always telling Kitty and me what to do—"

"Do not," Maggie said.

"Do too," Fiona said.

"Do NOT!"

"Do TOO!"

"STOP!" Sophie cried.

"No—let 'em go for it!"

That came from Colton Messik, who was suddenly standing three feet from them with the other two Fruit Loops.

"Fight!" Eddie shouted, face red. "Fight!"

Maggie turned on them like she was going to throw a punch. Sophie jumped on her back. Fiona got in front of them both and put up her hands.

"There isn't gonna be a fight, morons!" she said. "Go crawl back under your rock."

"She's dissin' you, man," Colton said to Tod. "You gonna let her get away with that?"

"She won't get away with it," Tod said. He turned like a basketball player doing a pivot, snapped his fingers in the air, and sauntered off toward the building with Colton and Eddie trailing him.

Colton walked backward and called to the Corn Flakes, "You heard him. He isn't kidding."

"Yeah, yeah," Fiona shouted back to him.

"Imbeciles," Maggie said.

"Definitely," Fiona said.

Sophie let all the air go out of her. At least they agreed on something. And for the moment, they seemed to have forgotten what it was they'd been about to fight about.

"So is it true you guys tried to kill each other in the hall this morning?" Harley said at the lunch table.

"Right in front of the office?" Gill said.

Nikki and Vette looked like they were totally convinced that it was the gospel truth and were prepared to take flight at the first sign of face-scratching and hair-pulling.

"It was out on the playground," Maggie said.

"Then you DID get in a fight?" Harley said.

"No, we almost did," Fiona said. She glared at Maggie.

Sophie groaned inside. So much for them forgetting why they were mad at each other.

Kitty smothered a gasp with her hand.

"What?" Fiona said. "Why are you freaking out?"

Kitty pointed toward the Corn Pops' table.

The Fruit Loops were sitting with them, talking and waving their arms all around like they were running for office.

No boys ever sat with girls. But the Fruit Loops looked like they were right at home.

Why not? Sophie thought. *They're all rich and popular and mean.*

Still, with the seven of them teaming up, it couldn't be good.

It couldn't be good at all.

That night after Zeke was tucked in, Mama went out to her Loom Room over the garage. When Sophie went downstairs to check out the flight food in the space kitchen, Daddy was in front of his computer again. Sophie wondered what could possibly be so inter-esting on there for hours on end.

When she came out of the kitchen with a neat stack of Mama's double-fudge brownies and a glass of milk, Daddy called from his study, "Hey, Soph. What are you up to?"

"Just having a little snack," Sophie said. She headed for the stairs.

"Come in here a minute."

Sophie turned reluctantly toward the study. Maybe she shouldn't have helped herself to quite so many brownies.

Daddy took one look at her plate and said, "A little snack? Were you planning to share that with Lacie?"

"No," Sophie said.

Daddy grinned. "I love that honesty. Lacie wouldn't eat those anyway. She's now decided that boys don't like her because she's fat."

"She's not fat."

"I know that, and you know that, but you can't convince her of that." Daddy nodded toward the recliner next to his desk. "Let's have at those brownies."

Sophie climbed into the big chair and tucked her feet up under her. She put the milk on Daddy's desk so they could both dunk.

"How's that science project coming along?" Daddy said. "You need any more info?"

Daddy had been as good as Boppa about helping the astronauts, only instead of showing them how to make things, he taught Maggie how to set up a system for keeping track of their data — that's what he called their results — on the computer. He even gave Kitty an offi-cial NASA clipboard so she'd feel more scientific when she was fol-lowing Fiona around the space station, writing down what Fiona told her to.

"I do have a question for you," Sophie said.

Daddy churned a brownie around in the milk and said, "Shoot."

"Do you ever have people on your crew disagreeing with each other?"

"Are you kidding? That's how we get to the truth of things, by debating. That's the way scientists work."

Sophie nodded in her most scientific way. "Are they ever mean to each other?"

"Some people might say that. Tempers can get pretty hot."

"What do you do then?"

Daddy chewed thoughtfully on another mouthful. So far he'd eaten three brownies to Sophie's one. They were going to need a milk refill soon.

"I tell people to go cool off," he said finally. "Then I get them back together and we look at the ideas again." Daddy grinned. "Sometimes I take a batch of your mother's cookies in with me. That almost never fails."

"Do you ever take a vote?" Sophie said.

"We vote on things like where to have lunch. Most of our decisions are made scientifically, though. It's whatever is best for the project we're working on. You want some more milk?"

Sophie nodded, and Daddy headed for the kitchen. He was whistling.

That was a scathingly brilliant conversation, Sophie thought.

"I put a little chocolate syrup in it," Daddy said as he set the glass down between them again.

Sophie was glad he hadn't brought two different glasses. Sharing was—well, it wasn't scientific, but it felt good.

"So what else you got on your mind?" he said.

"Well." Sophie formed her words carefully as she watched Daddy consume another brownie. He'd also brought another stack of those from the kitchen.

"Deep subject," Daddy said.

"I just would like to know — if — everything is okay with you and Mama."

Daddy stopped with a brownie soaking in the milk. He held it in there so long Sophie was surprised it didn't fall apart.

"You don't need to worry about that, Soph," he said.

"Then everything IS okay."

"It isn't perfect. But it's going to be okay, and you don't need to worry about it."

But from the look on Daddy's face, Sophie was more convinced than ever that she did need to worry about it. His cheeks looked like they were pinching toward his ears as he set the brownie on the plate, where it wilted in a puddle of milk.

"Soph," he said, "Mama is upset. But if you keep doing what you're doing, staying in the GATE program and making those good grades and not getting in trouble, she'll feel better. Deal?"

"Deal," Sophie said. But she didn't feel like eating any more brownies. "I think I should go to bed now," she told Daddy.

"Mama will come kiss you good night when she comes in."

Sophie hurried to her room and curled into her pillows and squeezed her eyes shut and wished she'd never asked Daddy that question. Because whatever wasn't "perfect" between Mama and him was because of her.

Captain Stella Stratos buried her face in her hands, but only for a moment. This was tragic, yes, but she had a space station to run, and a world to save. She had to sacrifice worrying about her personal problems for the good of the planet.

When that didn't do much to uncurl Sophie from her pillows, she closed her eyes again and imagined Jesus. She saw his kind eyes that understood stuff she didn't even get. His soft smile that was like Boppa's only even more pure. And his broad chest, like Daddy's, where the answers were hidden, was just a prayer away.

"Jesus, please," Sophie whispered. "I need to know how to keep Mama and Daddy from getting a divorce because I'm their problem child. And I have to keep the Corn Flakes from splitting up because of Maggie and Fiona — and ruining our whole science project and getting me kicked out of GATE. If I wait really patiently and listen for you to answer, will you tell me what to do to change everybody's mind? I figure you'll help me, because you always do."

Then she started to cry, straight into the pillows. When she heard Mama coming up the stairs, she pretended to be asleep. Seeing Sophie bawling would only upset her some more. She didn't want to imagine what would happen then.

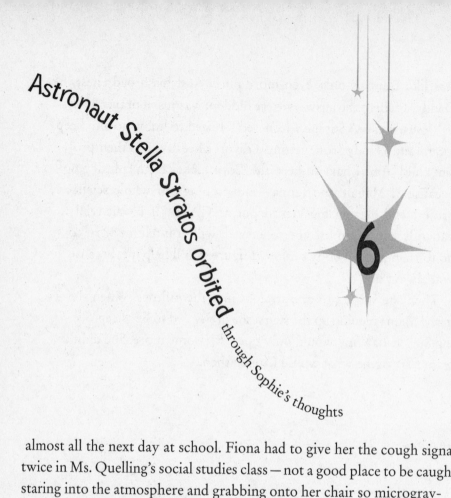

Astronaut Stella Stratos orbited *through Sophie's thoughts*

6

almost all the next day at school. Fiona had to give her the cough signal twice in Ms. Quelling's social studies class — not a good place to be caught staring into the atmosphere and grabbing onto her chair so microgravity wouldn't send her floating up to the ceiling.

But at least by the time the astronauts gathered in the space station that afternoon, Stella — and Sophie — had a plan.

She announced that they were having a crew meeting.

"Why?" Maggie said.

"Because she's the captain, Nimbus," Fiona said. "She can call a crew meeting any time she wants to."

"You ready for a snack, space travelers?" said a voice from below.

Sophie leaned over the railing to see Kateesha on the ground, hooking a plastic bag over the crook in the robot-arm cane.

"Beam it up," Sophie called down.

"Roger, *Freedom 4*," Kateesha said.

Kitty giggled. "That's so cool."

"Thank you, Huntsville," Sophie said.

"Why did you call her 'Huntsville'?" Maggie said. "Her name's Kateesha."

"Our home base is in Huntsville," Sophie told her. "That's who we communicate with while we're in outer space."

They helped themselves to cookies shaped like moons and stars and rockets. Kitty giggled every time she popped one into her mouth.

"Do they eat these in space?" Maggie said.

"They do now," Fiona said.

"If I could have your attention," Captain Stella said. "Now that our space station is almost completed, we must come to a decision about comparing gravity to microgravity. I would like for each one of you to present your reasons why you want it done one way or the other, and then we will vote on which idea sounds the best.

"We'll start with you, Nimbus. Please tell us your idea — "

The words began to thud from Astronaut Nimbus's mouth. "I think we need something besides just building the space station to compare. The only difference is that things don't stay put in microgravity and they do here." She furrowed her forehead. "That means there's nothing for me to write down. I say we add some plants and see how they grow here and how they grow in space. I'll do that. I know about gardening. My mom and I — "

"It sounds like it's all about you," Astronaut Jupiter said.

"I can't help it if I came up with the best idea."

"What about yours, Luna?" Sophie said.

There was silence.

"Kitty," Sophie whispered.

"Oh — yeah — I'm Luna, huh?" Kitty giggled. "I'm Fiona's assistant, so I'm going to vote for whatever she says."

"Not fair," Maggie said.

"It is too fair," Fiona said. "She's taking her job very seriously."

"So what is your idea?" Captain Stella said to Jupiter.

Fiona pushed the hair out of her face. "If we try to grow plants out here, they'll freeze at night. I say we just stick with the space station."

"But then I don't get to be the record keeper," Maggie said. "It's not fair."

"It isn't about what's fair," Sophie said. "It's about what's best for the project."

"Then let's vote," Fiona said.

"All for Maggie's idea, raise your hand," Sophie said.

Maggie's arm went straight up in the air.

"All for Fiona's idea?"

Kitty and Fiona raised their hands, and Kitty grabbed Fiona's, the way Sophie had seen people running for president do with their wives on TV.

"Not fair," Maggie said.

"How is that not fair?" Fiona said. "It's two against one."

"Sophie didn't vote."

They all looked at Captain Stella, who swallowed a large lump of a moon cookie.

"Whose side are you on?" Maggie said.

"Like I said, I want what's best for the project," Sophie said. She swallowed again. *How does Daddy do this every single day?* she thought.

"So vote," Maggie said.

"Okay. I think Astronaut Jupiter's idea is the best. Only we could make it so that — "

"Not fair."

Fiona turned to Maggie, nostrils in a record-breaking flare.

"You know what, NIMbus?" she said. "You're just mad because you didn't get your own way. That isn't very scientific."

"This whole project is just gonna be dumb now," Maggie said.

And with that final thudding sentence, she snatched up her backpack and disappeared down the ladder. The other three Corn Flakes waited until they heard her land heavily in "Huntsville" before they said a word.

Fiona let out a huge relief-sigh. "Good riddance, is what I say."

"Me, too," Kitty said. "She's way too bossy."

But Sophie shook her head. "Who's going to keep the records?"

"We won't have any records, remember?" Fiona said.

"I was going to tell you guys how we could do it so she'd have stuff to write down," Sophie said, "but she didn't even wait for me to finish."

"Luna can do it," Fiona said.

Kitty's face froze up. "Me? I can't spell that good and my handwriting stinks."

"It doesn't matter . . . ," Sophie started to tell her.

And then she stopped. Fiona's eyes went into slits, and Sophie felt her stomach churn. She had never seen her best friend look so much like a Corn Pop. This Fiona was wearing a face that said, *Don't mess with me. I'll get my way.*

"The only problem," Fiona said, in a voice that matched her eyes, "is that Maggie took all of our plans with her. I hope she doesn't try to sell them to the enemy."

"We have enemies?" Kitty said.

As Astronaut Jupiter went on to explain that there were always intergallactic villains flying around at light speed, Captain Stella Stratos closed her eyes.

We have had a mutiny, just as I feared, she thought. What's to be done? When the head of NASA, Mrs. Utley, finds out that Astronaut Nimbus has left the program, we will be called in for questioning. I do not want to tell her that there has been too much fighting among the Expedition Crew. That violates the code of the Corn Flake Society: we will not leave anyone out. Captain Stratos looked out into deep space. *I feel responsible for Astronaut Nimbus. What is she to do for a project? And can we save the planet without her?*

Sophie's stomach churned even more. And what about Fiona? Why was she suddenly like the people Sophie always daydreamed her way away from?

Captain Stella put her hands up to her space helmet and checked its arrangement on her head. She was certainly glad that she had an appointment with the NASA psychologist the next day. Scientist Peter Topping would know exactly what to do.

Mama went up to the Loom Room again after supper that night, and even though Daddy made popcorn and invited everybody to watch *Finding Nemo* on video with him after they did their homework, Sophie felt like there was a big old hole in the family room where Mama should have been. Lacie wanted to watch *Clueless* for about the seventy-fifth time, and when Daddy said "unh-uh" (and Zeke howled the longest "NO-O-O" in history), Lacie stomped upstairs and slammed her bedroom door.

Daddy looked at Sophie over the head of Zeke, who was still hollering, and said, "You're the only sane person left in this family."

Even that didn't wipe out Sophie's worries.

Mama made them worse the next morning by being way quiet while everybody was getting ready for school. She didn't even say much when Zeke put his socks on his ears instead of his feet and stuck a raisin into each nostril.

I wonder if she's daydreaming, Sophie thought. *I hope she's not imagining leaving us.*

The pang in her chest went straight through to her backbone. She couldn't blow this science project, or Mama would get upset. She couldn't do anything that would let Mama go. That just couldn't happen. Sophie climbed off her stool at the snack bar and knelt down beside Zeke.

"I'll put his shoes and socks on him, Mama," she said.

Mama mumbled a "thank you" and went back to the lunch boxes, where she was making peanut butter and jelly sandwiches again.

Between that and the memory of Fiona with slanted eyes and sneery voice, it was impossible not to let Captain Stella Stratos take over during the school day. Sophie imagined Jesus, too, and she begged him again to help her fix things. But he just kept smiling his kind smile and didn't give her any answers.

In second period, Ms. Quelling made them read, and most of the class had their faces in their social studies books, except for the Fruit Loops. Tod was acting like he was reading, but Sophie could see him giving directions to the other two Loops with his sharp little eyes. Colton kept leaning under his desk like he was trying to find something, and when he seemed to get his hands on it, he slipped it to Eddie. Sophie was expecting them to take the whole class hostage any minute.

That's exactly the sort of thing we need to save the planet from, Captain Stella Stratos thought. *The secret plans of Moron-oids who want to take over the universe and make people bow down to them and feed them Cheetos.*

Captain Stella adjusted her glasses. She was going to have to be prepared to evacuate the room when the Moron-oids opened fire with their secret space weapons. If only she knew what they were. It was hard to defend a planet against the unknown. So far, all she had been able to figure out from their presence was that they had brains they seldom used except to humiliate the citizens of earth. And that they had a peculiar smell. And that they could not be trusted.

She needed to get closer now, where she could possibly gather data.

Stella crept in clandestine fashion around the back of the Huntsville control room, keeping out of sight of the Moron-oids. As she drew closer to their corner, she paused, making certain that she wasn't seen. She glanced at her official Freedom 4 watch. It was ten hundred hours. She would need to make a note of that in her report.

But in the instant she took her eyes from the Moron-oids, the three space villains had gotten off a shot. Several small green projectiles were thrust from a tube planted firmly in Moron-oid Eddie's nose.

Those could be weapons of mass destruction! Captain Stella thought. With the lightning speed of a finely-tuned scientific mind, she made a decision. Diving from her place against the wall, she hurled herself forward and grasped for the green bullet that was even then piercing through the air. It didn't matter that she herself could be mortally wounded. She couldn't let anyone else be hurt.

The bullet hit the palm of her hand, and she curled her fingers around it just as gravity pushed her to the floor. Even before she hit the ground she could feel the tiny green object giving way to a soft mush in her hand. It could be some form of biological warfare —

Or it could be a pea. Sophie sat on the floor, right at the feet of Julia Cummings, and stared at her open palm. A green mass was squished right in the middle.

"Gross me out!" Julia said.

"What is going on?" Ms. Quelling called out from her desk.

Sophie could hardly hear her over the racket that was coming from the Fruit Loops' corner. Their monkey-laughter shrieked right up to the ozone layer. Eddie fell out of his desk.

Ms. Quelling stood over Sophie, looking down between two thick curtains

of bronze-colored hair.

"Sophie," she said. *"What on earth?"* Then she looked at Julia, eyebrows up.

"I don't know," Julia said. "She just threw herself down here like some kind of freak." She put up both hands, spreading out her fingers-with-the-Valentine-red-fingernails. "I didn't do anything to her, I swear."

"All right, get up off the ground, for starters," Ms. Quelling said to Sophie.

She didn't appear to notice that Eddie was still rolling on the floor, his face as red as Julia's manicure. By the time Sophie got to her feet, she was aware that the whole class had their faces in their books and their eyes over the tops of the pages on her. The entire room seemed to be holding its breath.

"What in the world were you doing?" Ms. Quelling said. Her forehead was twisted into a question mark.

"I was catching this," Sophie said, opening her hand. "Eddie was shooting them out of his nose."

Julia coiled up and slapped the red nails over her mouth.

"It's a good thing I did, too," Sophie said to her, "because it was headed straight for the side of your face."

Ms. Quelling turned to the Fruit Loops. "Is this true, boys? Where is Eddie?"

Tod and Colton both pointed calmly to the floor.

"Eddie! Get up!" Ms. Quelling said.

"I can't!" Eddie said. "I think I laughed myself to death."

I hope so, Sophie thought.

"Is this your pea, Eddie?" Ms. Quelling said.

That did it. The class let out its held-back breath in one enormous burst of hysteria. Ms. Quelling closed her eyes, and Sophie could see her trying not to join in.

"All right, go wash your hand, Sophie," Ms. Quelling said. "Eddie, come up to my desk, and bring your peas with you."

"He doesn't have them," Sophie said. "Colton does."

Ms. Quelling gave Sophie a pointy look, as if Sophie hadn't just made her life easier by giving her all the information she needed. "I will talk to *you* later," she said.

Later didn't happen right away, which meant Sophie couldn't think about anything else through the rest of her morning classes except that Ms. Quelling was after her again. By lunchtime, Sophie could barely choke down her peanut butter and jelly sandwich.

"I don't see why you would get in trouble," Kitty said. "You were just trying to save Julia."

"The question is, why?" Fiona said.

Maggie would probably have jumped right in and reminded Fiona that the Corn Flakes tried to protect everybody from harm. But Maggie hadn't hung out with them all day. Right now she was sitting alone all the way at the other end of the table, past the Wheaties, putting one tortilla chip after another into her mouth like letters into a mail slot.

"Uh-oh," Kitty said. "Here comes Ms. Quelling. I think you're busted, Sophie."

Ms. Quelling stopped at the end of the table, forehead twisted into that question mark thing like it had been there since second period. Fiona squeezed Sophie's hand.

"You were right, Sophie," Ms. Quelling said. "Eddie and Colton were doing their boy thing. I've dealt with them."

"And Tod?" Sophie said.

"What does Tod have to do with it?"

"He put them up to it. I saw him."

"Which brings me to why you were lurking on that side of the room in the first place, Sophie," Ms. Quelling said. "You were supposed to be reading."

Sophie didn't answer. Ms. Quelling would never understand about a scientific thing.

"Never mind," Ms. Quelling said. "I know what you were up to. Now that Julia and B.J. and Anne-Stuart have changed and you can't blame everything on them anymore, you're looking for ways to get the boys in trouble."

"I wasn't doing that!" Sophie said.

"Trust me, Ms. Quelling," Fiona said, her gray eyes wide and serious. "I know Sophie. She would never do that."

"Thank you, Fiona," Ms. Quelling said coldly. "When Sophie needs a character witness, I'm sure she'll call you." She lowered her sights on Sophie again like she was aiming a rifle. "I'm going to let it go this time, but from now on, you'd better leave those boys alone. Don't think you can do this kind of thing and stay in the GATE program."

They don't leave us alone! Sophie wanted to say.

As Ms. Quelling strode out of the cafeteria—amid calls from the Corn Pops of "Hi, Ms. Quelling! Love you!"—Kitty turned frightened eyes on Sophie.

"Why does she hate you so much?"

"Because Sophie has proved her wrong twice before about her little teacher's pets," Fiona said. "She can't tolerate being wrong."

"I know what 'tolerate' means," Kitty said. "You should leave them alone, Sophie."

"I'm not doing anything to them! They're the ones doing it all!"

"Besides," Fiona said, "we vowed we could handle them, and we will."

"How can we do that when we can't even talk to them?" Kitty said.

Nobody had an answer for that.

"I can't figure out why they're all of a sudden picking on you," Fiona said to Sophie. "Up 'til, like, two weeks ago, they acted like we didn't even exist."

"I wish they still did," Kitty said.

"Let's just pretend THEY don't exist," Sophie said. "That's how we'll handle them. It isn't bad to leave them out and not be friendly to them and stuff. They're boys."

Besides—there was the space station to think about. They had to give a progress report in science that afternoon, and Maggie had their plan.

"I'm just gonna go ask her for it," Fiona said when they got to P.E.

Sophie had a sudden vision of another almost-fistfight right there on the playground.

"No — I'll think of something — scientific," she said. "I'm the captain."

A basketball bounced by, and as Fiona turned to run after it, she murmured to Sophie, "Pretty soon, it's just going to be the original Corn Flakes again." The smile she gave Sophie wasn't Fiona-luscious.

Sophie's thoughts went straight for Captain Stella, but she was barely able to get her into focus when the basketball suddenly knocked her in the head and set her on her tail on the concrete. It was Maggie who pulled her up and asked her if she was okay.

"I'm fine," Sophie said.

"Let me look at your eyes," Maggie said.

Sophie stared as Maggie squinted critically into her face.

"I don't think you have a concussion," she said.

"How do you know, Nimbus?" Fiona said.

"I have a first aid card. My mom and I went to a class together."

"Wow," Kitty said. "That's cool."

First aid. Suddenly, Sophie had an idea.

"I know you're upset about my decision yesterday, Nimbus," she said. "But I want you to consider the whole crew. With your medical knowledge, you could actually save our lives if we got into trouble."

Maggie hesitated for a minute, pressing her lips together. "I would need to put my first aid kit in the space station," she said.

"Of course," Captain Stella said. "Anything you need. Right, Expedition Crew?"

Kitty looked at Fiona. Even though Fiona pulled her lips into a knot, she finally nodded.

Sophie was feeling better about everything when she got into the Suburban that afternoon so Mama could take her to see Dr. Peter. At LAST. And when Mama smiled at her, she felt even better.

"Hey, Dream Girl," Mama said. "I want to thank you for helping with Zeke this morning. I know I haven't been myself lately, and you gave me a little lift."

Does that mean you aren't leaving us? Sophie wanted to say. Instead, she said, "I'll help any time you want, Mama. I could give him his bath and read him books and clean up his room — "

Mama gave her a blank stare before she smiled again. "Don't overdo it, Sophie," she said. "You'll have me thinking you're trying to butter me up for something!" She squeezed Sophie's knee. "Now — how was your day? Anything exciting happen?"

The incident with Eddie and the peas ran through Sophie's head, chased by the scene with Ms. Quelling in the cafeteria. She would tell Mama about that later, when she knew she was completely better. When she started making good lunches again and coming to tuck Sophie in at night.

But Sophie did bring it up with Dr. Peter the minute she was settled in on his window seat and had one of his face pillows on her lap. She chose the one with the fuzzy blue hair so she could comb her fingers through it and not chew her own hair while she talked.

"Whoa, Sophie-Lophie-Loodle," Dr. Peter said. "Start from the beginning. Tell me all about this Captain Stella Stratos." His twinkly blue eyes shone through the lenses of his wire-rimmed glasses. It was one of about a thousand things she liked about him. He wore glasses, too, and he was still about the most awesome grown-up she knew.

Sophie launched into a detailed account of Captain Stella and the space station and her recent issues with her crew. The whole time, Dr. Peter watched her and nodded his head of cut-short, reddish brown hair. When she was finished, Dr. Peter picked up the face pillow with the orange puffs of hair that came out of its nostrils.

"Sounds like our Loodle is going off to Sophie World in school again," he said to it. "What do you think?"

The pillow nodded. Dr. Peter looked at Sophie. "Why is that?"

"Because we have to get our project done. It's very complex. It requires a lot of concentration."

"You haven't by any chance forgotten your agreement with your dad, have you?"

"You mean only going into Sophie World when I'm filming?" Sophie sighed. "I am filming. AND I'm imagining Jesus. But it's not helping."

"Okay," Dr. Peter said. "You want to do a treasure hunt and find out why?"

That was another reason she liked Dr. Peter. He never even looked like he thought she was loony tunes.

"Okay," she said. "Only, could we make it like exploring outer space instead? I'm really into that right now."

"Of course. Silly me," he said. "Now — I want you to close your eyes and imagine you're going through space in your capsule."

That was easy. Stars and planets began to zip by in her mind.

"Now, as you know, Captain," he went on, "sometimes meteors go through space and leave a trail of debris on things they hit."

"Is any of it going to hit my capsule?" Sophie said.

"It may. If that happens, you need to stop and see what it was and how much damage it has done. Then you can decide if you can fix it."

"Yes, sir," Sophie said.

"All right, proceed through space and let me know when something collides with your craft."

Sophie opened one eye. "What if I ask Jesus not to let anything hit me?"

"You can ask that. But it might be better to ask him to keep you from being damaged when something hits you. Outer space is filled with flying objects for a reason we don't even understand —

even though we're scientists. Being strong enough to handle them all is what we need to ask for."

Sophie closed her eyes again, and almost immediately she imagined something hitting square in the middle of the space capsule's window.

"Reduce speed, Captain, and let's examine it."

"Do I open my eyes?" Sophie said.

"Whatever helps you see best."

Sophie kept her eyes squeezed shut and let herself imagine the big rock that had split apart against the space-worthy glass.

"What do you think it is?" Dr. Peter said.

"I can't tell."

She could picture Dr. Peter's nose wrinkling to push up his glasses. "It looks to me like a piece of a family," he said.

"A family? You mean, like, people?"

"It's more like an idea of a family."

"Oh," Sophie said. "And it came apart."

Suddenly, she felt squirmy, and her chest hurt.

"Permission to move on, Huntsville," Sophie said. "I have decided my capsule wasn't damaged."

"Loodle," Dr. Peter said. He was using his soft come-back-to-earth voice.

Sophie hugged the pillow to her chest and opened her eyes.

"I don't want to talk about families falling apart, Dr. Peter," she said.

"Is that because you're afraid your family is falling apart?"

Sophie nodded.

"You want to tell me about it?"

No, she didn't. But the words came out anyway, in one big blurt.

"Zeke is acting out all over the place like he's Terrible Two again," she said. "Lacie is being all weird about boys. Daddy says I'm the only sane one left in the family."

"What about your father? Is he being 'all weird'?"

Sophie shook her head. "We're getting along better than ever in my whole entire life." She hugged the pillow until its nose dug into her stomach. She knew what Dr. Peter's next question was going to be.

"And how about your mama?" he said.

"I think she's gonna leave us! She hardly laughs or talks, and she acts like she's always mad at Daddy. And it's all my fault!"

"Your fault?" Dr. Peter said. "You want to tell me why you think that?"

"Daddy told me if I kept making good grades and staying out of trouble, she would feel better. That's why I didn't tell her about what happened today. She might just pack her suitcase and go. I would hate it without her. She's my mama!"

Sophie didn't realize until then that she was crying. Dr. Peter handed her a Kleenex out of a box with moons and stars on it.

Sophie plastered one over her eyes and cried into it some more. Dr. Peter just waited. When she looked up at him, he was studying her carefully.

"You know, Loodle," he said, "I almost never tell you that you're wrong."

"Are you going to now?" Sophie said.

"I am." He leaned forward. "You are so wrong about anything between your mother and father being your fault. Or Zeke's, or Lacie's."

"But I don't want her to leave for any reason. I'm trying to fix it. I'm helping with Zeke when he starts acting like a little brat, and I'm not fighting with Lacie. But I already miss Mama, and she isn't even gone yet."

Dr. Peter nodded. "Do you feel like she's gone because she isn't with you like she used to be with you?"

"Yes!" Sophie said.

"You know something, Loodle?" he said. "You sometimes know things about people they haven't even figured out about themselves."

Sophie felt the pain in her chest again. "Then she is going to leave. I have to stop her!"

"Now hang on," Dr. Peter said. "All I'm saying is that you seem to understand that she is taking a little mental trip right now, just like you do when you get scared about things and go into Sophie World."

"What's she scared of?" Sophie said.

"That I can't tell you. But I think you're the best person in the house to understand about wanting to escape."

Sophie straightened her shoulders. "I can help her, then. I'll give her a signal when she starts drifting off, like Fiona coughs when she sees me zoning out in school."

Dr. Peter's face grew serious. "I don't want you to try to fix your mother, okay, Loodle? First of all, that isn't your job. It's God's."

"But I keep asking him to fix it and he doesn't!"

"I think he's working on it. In fact, I'm sure of it. What do you say we let him do his job and you do yours? Just like the astronauts on your crew."

"But what's my job?" Sophie said.

Dr. Peter's eyes twinkled again. "I think it's time to get to know Jesus a little bit better so you can see how God handles stuff like this."

"Back to the Bible," Sophie said.

"You're brilliant," Dr. Peter said, handing her a piece of paper with Bible verses written on it. "That must be why they made you captain of the spaceship. Now remember, read the story and imagine yourself playing one of the parts."

"I can do that."

"Yes, you can. And I'm going to give you a little hint — pay attention to what the little kid does and what Jesus does with that."

"Roger," Sophie said.

She wasn't crying when she left Dr. Peter's office. She had the Bible verses tucked in her pocket, and a new idea tucked in her head.

It's like another mission. God is Huntsville, and I'm flying the space capsule.

She was almost smiling when she met Daddy in the waiting room. One look at his face, though, and the desire to grin shattered like a piece of space debris. His mouth was in a tight line she hadn't seen there since the last time she was in big trouble.

Daddy didn't say anything until they got into the truck, and Sophie

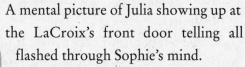

didn't ask him any questions. But as soon as he pulled out into Hampton traffic, he said, "I thought we had a deal."

Sophie readjusted her glasses to peer at him. "We do!" she said. "I'm not even making any C's right now."

"You will be soon if you pull another stunt like you did in school today."

A mental picture of Julia showing up at the LaCroix's front door telling all flashed through Sophie's mind.

"Ms. Quelling called to tell me that you almost tackled somebody to catch a pea some kid shot out of a straw, just to get the kid in trouble."

"That isn't what happened!" Sophie said.

"I know that isn't what happened. What happened was you got so wrapped up in one of your daydreams you started acting it out, and suddenly there you were, sprawled out on the floor with a smashed vegetable in your hand." Daddy pulled up to a red light and lowered his eyebrows at her. "That's what happened, right?"

"Yes!" Sophie said. "But it won't happen again. I promise."

"Do you need a little reminder? Do I need to take the camera away for a while?"

Sophie tried to remain calm, although she had to clutch the door handle to do it.

"No," she said. "Dr. Peter helped me with that today."

Daddy was quiet for a few blocks. Sophie chewed her hair and swung her legs against the seat. Her feet didn't touch the floor in Daddy's truck as it was, and she was feeling smaller by the minute.

"It isn't just about your grades, Soph," Daddy said. "I told you I didn't want you upsetting your mother."

"Does she know about this?" Sophie said.

"No. Ms. Quelling called me at work."

"She interrupted you trying to save the planet to tell you that?"

Sophie thought she saw the corners of Daddy's mouth twitch.

"Yeah," he said. "And I think she enjoyed it." He shot Sophie a Daddy-look. "But that doesn't mean you didn't mess up."

"Am I going to get a punishment?" she said.

"Definitely."

Sophie felt her heart take a dive. It probably wasn't going to be as bad as banishment from the planet, but still.

"Tonight, after you finish your homework," Daddy said, "you have to bring a glass of milk and exactly twelve cookies to my study and stay there until they're all gone."

"I can endure that."

"Is that a Fiona word?" Daddy said.

"Yes, sir," Sophie said.

She waited until she got up to her room after supper to really sigh, so Daddy wouldn't think that she thought she was getting off easy. The feeling didn't last long, though. Fiona called, puffing like a bull on the other end of the line.

"Huntsville, we have a problem," she said.

"What is it, Jupiter?" Sophie said.

"I just went up to *Freedom 4* to get my backpack I left up there after we were working today — and the robot arm was totally torn off."

Sophie gasped. "Did the wind do it?"

"There was no wind today."

"Didn't we attach it right?"

"It didn't happen by itself," Fiona said. "Boppa went up there and looked at it. He said somebody tore it off!"

Sophie's tongue went stiff. "Who would do that? Oh — it was Rory and Isabella, huh?"

"No — they were at the library with Kateesha all afternoon. Besides, I know who did this, and so do you."

"I do?"

"It was so Maggie. She brought costumes today, by the way — "

"Are they amazing?"

"They look just like the pictures," Fiona said. "But that isn't the point."

Sophie could almost see Fiona's eyes going into Corn Pop slits.

"She was even pretty decent when she and Kitty were up in the space station with me," Fiona said, "but that was just an act. She's still mad because we didn't do it her way."

Sophie was shaking her head as if Fiona could see her through the phone. "It doesn't make sense. If she messed it up, it would ruin her grade, too."

"That's just it. She thinks she's going to tell us how to fix it and she'll get her way because our way didn't work, and when we get a good grade she'll say it was all because of her. We could even get taken out of GATE for not doing more work than her." Fiona gave a hard little laugh. "But I have news for her. Boppa already fixed it. He said it was something we couldn't do and he'll explain it to Mrs. Utley. I'm sure glad Ms. Quelling isn't our science teacher." Fiona finally took a breath. "So what are you going to do now?"

"Me?"

"You're the captain. You need to have a plan, or Maggie is going to keep doing things until she ruins it for all of us. I think you should call a meeting of just you, me, and Luna, and tell us what you want us to do."

Sophie mumbled something and hung up and closed her eyes. Jesus showed up right away, looking at her with kind eyes.

"Is this your job or mine?" she whispered to him.

He didn't answer, of course, but it did make her think of the Bible story Dr. Peter had told her to read. That was supposed to be about the Mama Mission, but she needed some help with this mission or it was going to fall completely apart.

Sophie pulled her Bible out and propped up against her pile of plump pillows. She noted that she and Dr. Peter were both into big cushions. Another reason she liked him so much.

It wasn't hard to find John 6, verses 1 through 13. Since before Christmas, Dr. Peter had her read a Bible story almost every time she saw him and she was getting good at finding her way around.

Jesus crossed to the far shore of the Sea of Galilee, she read, *and a great crowd of people followed him because they saw the miraculous signs he had performed on the sick.*

Sophie could already imagine herself as one of them. Any minute now, he would perform a miraculous sign for her and fix this whole space-station dilemma. She got a picture in her head of herself in a little purple robe and a rope belt and sandals.

When Jesus looked up and saw a great crowd coming toward him, he said to Philip, "Where shall we buy bread for these people to eat?" He asked this only to test him, for he already had in mind what he was going to do.

Sophie was glad she hadn't imagined herself as Philip. She didn't know the answer to that question.

Philip answered him, "Eight months' wages would not buy enough bread for each one to have a bite!"

Another of his disciples, Andrew, Simon Peter's brother, spoke up. "Here is a boy with five small barley loaves and two small fish, but how far will they go among so many?"

Sophie thought that must be the little kid Dr. Peter had mentioned. She decided it was okay if she made the boy a girl. Quickly she created a picture in her mind of her sandal-footed self, holding up a couple of fish and five very small loaves of bread. She wasn't sure what barley was, but she mentally sprinkled some seeds on top of the loaves and let it go at that. The important thing was the feeling she was already getting in her chest, like her heart was so afraid Jesus wouldn't like what she had to offer. But after all, she was the only one in the whole crowd who had bothered to bring a lunch.

Jesus said, "Have the people sit down." There was plenty of grass in that place, and the men sat down, about five thousand of them. Jesus then took the loaves, gave thanks, and distributed to those who were seated as much as they wanted. He did the same with the fish.

Sophie breathed a huge sigh. He liked the lunch, or he wouldn't be giving thanks for it. She took a few seconds to imagine Jesus holding the little rolls up toward heaven and saying, "God is great, God is good. Now we thank you for this food." The smell of them wafted down to her nose. She was starting to get hungry.

It was one of those all-you-can-eat things, Sophie thought. All Daddy could eat was enough for about three people. If there were five thousand like him, that was a lot of food. Sophie closed her eyes and saw it all, steaming loaves being passed to the ones in the back who thought they wouldn't get even a crumb. Herself running up and down the rows, grass tickling her stuck-out toes as she handed out basket after basket of fish until everyone was groaning because they'd completely pigged out.

Opening her eyes, she continued. *When they had all had enough to eat, he said to his disciples, "Gather the pieces that are left over. Let nothing be wasted." So they gathered them* — with Sophie helping — *and filled twelve baskets with the pieces of the five barley loaves left over by those who had eaten.*

Sophie closed the Bible on her lap, but she kept her eyes open. The story was as clear as if it had happened right down at Buckroe Beach, but she knew her forehead was wrinkled into about five thousand folds.

What's that got to do with Mama — *or the Freedom 4* — *or any other problem I have?* she thought. *I don't get it.*

She wished Dr. Peter were there so he could explain it to her. With Fiona and Kitty expecting a plan tomorrow morning, she didn't have time to wait two weeks for her next appointment. She ran her finger down the wrinkles in her forehead as she tried to imagine his voice, coaching her. All that came were the words he'd already said to her, that afternoon.

Pay attention to what the little kid does and what Jesus does with that.

Sophie went back to her imagination. The little kid was her. What had she done?

"I gave up my lunch," she said out loud. "It wasn't that much, but it was all Mama had packed for me. That must have been the Bible-days version of peanut butter and jelly sandwiches."

She dived back in. What had Jesus done with it?

Du-uh, she thought. *He fed, like, a bazillion people. He put his hands up with the bread and the fish in them and he gave thanks. And whammo—it was enough for a feast.*

Sophie gnawed at her hair. Was she supposed to take lunch for the Corn Flakes tomorrow? No, that couldn't be it. What else had Dr. Peter said about God?

What do you say we let him do his job and you do yours?

"Okay, so I bring one sandwich and he makes it enough for the whole cafeteria. No—la-ame."

Sophie devoured several split ends before she gave up and went downstairs to take the twelve cookies and one glass of milk to Daddy. She was tempted to ask him what he would do, but she decided that wasn't the best move. She wasn't supposed to try to fix Mama, but she didn't want to make her worse. If Mama found out there was trouble among the Corn Flakes and they might fail their science project if they didn't make it better, she would definitely be upset.

On the way down the steps, Sophie switched back to Jesus. *I guess I'm back to "you show me my job and I'll do it, and I'll let you do yours."*

And could you please hurry up?

The next morning Sophie got a ride with Daddy instead of taking the bus so she could get to school way early. The sun wasn't shining except for a blur in the gray clouds, struggling to seep through, and there was frost on everything. Sophie found Kitty and Fiona back-stage in the cafeteria, where they always met in bad weather, sitting in the middle of some old set pieces that they had pulled together to make a closed-off place.

Kitty jumped like somebody had popped a balloon when Sophie said, "Hi!" and she banged her head on a wooden tree. Fiona put her finger up to her lips.

"We're trying to keep a low profile," she whispered.

"We're also being very quiet," Kitty said.

Sophie nodded solemnly and slipped in between them. She wasn't even worried about floor dust getting on her khakis. This was serious stuff, and so far, Jesus hadn't given her so much as a hint of a plan.

"So what are we going to do?" Fiona said, voice low.

"We don't even know if it was really Maggie who broke the robot arm," Sophie said.

"I know," Fiona said.

"Can we prove it?"

Fiona's dark eyebrows squeezed together over her nose. "You mean, like, fingerprints or something?"

"We have to be scientific about it," Sophie said. "Besides, if we accuse her and it turns out she didn't do it, we could get into big trouble."

Fiona folded her arms stubbornly across her chest. "I still say it's Maggie. It has her name all over it. And how are we going to protect our project with her still involved in it?"

Sophie nibbled at the ends of her braids.

"The only way is to get rid of her," Fiona said.

"Like throw her over the side of the tree house?" Kitty said. Her eyes were bulging like a terrified bullfrog's.

"Hello! No!" Fiona put her hand over her mouth and looked toward the opening in the curtain.

"What?" Sophie said.

"I just don't want Maggie to hear us. You know she'll be looking for us any minute." She leaned in, and so did Kitty and

Sophie. "I mean, we have to prove she did it and then Mrs. Utley will take her off the project."

Sophie knew what to say now. "It's not our job to prove Maggie did it. Our job is to show how microgravity is different."

"And how are we going to make sure it doesn't get sabotaged?" Fiona said.

"Does that mean 'torn up'?" Kitty said.

Fiona had barely nodded when Sophie heard a voice thudding from the direction of the cafeteria door.

"Sophie? Fiona? You guys in here?"

"So what's the plan?" Fiona whispered.

"I'll get back to you," Sophie squeaked back.

"But we can't talk about it with her around," Fiona said.

"We could pass notes," Kitty said. "We used to do it all the time when I was a Corn Pop."

"I would get caught," Sophie said. "I can't do anything without getting caught. It's a curse."

"You guys?" Maggie's voice was getting louder and closer. According to Sophie's calculations, she would be on the stage in five seconds.

"I'll take that job," Fiona whispered. "If you get any ideas, just write them down and stick them in my pocket between classes. Then I'll put together a list."

Four, three, two, one —

"In here, Nimbus!" Sophie called out.

Maggie stuck her head through the opening in the curtain. Sophie hoped they didn't all look as guilty as she felt.

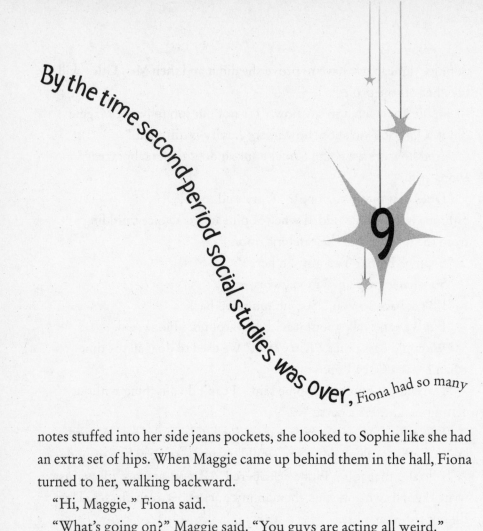

By the time second-period social studies was over, Fiona had so many notes stuffed into her side jeans pockets, she looked to Sophie like she had an extra set of hips. When Maggie came up behind them in the hall, Fiona turned to her, walking backward.

"Hi, Maggie," Fiona said.

"What's going on?" Maggie said. "You guys are acting all weird." Kitty shot Sophie a whimpering look. Fiona's glance clearly said, *Uh-oh*.

"See?" Maggie said to Sophie. "It's like you have some kinda secret or something."

Suddenly, Sophie felt like she was one of the Corn Pops, about to squeal out, *Oh, no, Maggie, we would never keep a secret from you.*

It made her want to hiss at herself. This definitely wasn't the job she was supposed to be doing. She linked her arm through Maggie's and held on as they walked, even though Maggie stiffened up as if Sophie were trying to freeze-dry her.

"We didn't want to upset you," Sophie said. "But you should know."

Fiona suddenly sounded like she was choking to death. Kitty was now whimpering out loud.

"Know what?" Maggie said.

They stopped outside the door to the computer room.

"Somebody tore the robot arm off the *Freedom 4* yesterday," Sophie said.

"Who?" Maggie said.

Fiona gave Sophie a what-are-you-doing stare.

"We don't know who did it," Sophie said. "But we have to protect the project."

"You mean, like, set up a stakeout?"

The whining, whimpering, and choking all stopped. The three other Corn Flakes stared at Maggie.

"Tell me some more," Sophie said.

"Write it in a note," Fiona said. "The bell's gonna ring."

Not that Mrs. Yacanovich ever noticed people coming in late. It took her half the period just to call the roll and get people to stop hollering things across the room to one another long enough to give the assignment. That gave all the Corn Flakes a chance to whip off notes. The only thing Sophie was worried about then was getting them mixed up with the ones the Corn Pops were delivering to each other. They actually had it down to a science, Sophie noticed. Julia could write a half-page letter and get replies back from Willoughby, B.J., and Anne-Stuart in the time it took Sophie to get one folded. They'd obviously had a lot more practice.

Maggie wrote a note to Sophie, folded it up into a perfect triangle, and dropped it next to her computer. Before Sophie could even reach for it, Colton came out of nowhere and snatched it up. He shot it like a basketball toward the corner trash can.

Fortunately, Colton was no basketball player. The note missed by about half a classroom and landed right on top of Anne-Stuart's computer monitor. Good fortune was with them again, because Anne-Stuart was, of course, blowing her nose at the time, and didn't get to it before Kitty leaped from her chair and grabbed it. She looked at Anne-Stuart and said, "Sorry — wrong address!" Then she giggled and flipped around in time to avoid Mrs. Y. who was chasing Eddie Wornom down the aisle. He had her grade book.

But Sophie saw that more trouble was coming Kitty's way in the form of Tod.

"Kitty!" she hissed. Although how Kitty was supposed to hear her over the classroom racket was beyond her.

When Tod kept dodging stuck-out feet and elbows with eyes riveted on that note in Kitty's hand, Sophie scrambled up to her knees in the chair and waved her arms.

"Give it up, LaCroix," said a male voice at her elbow. "You'll never get off the ground."

Sophie whipped her head around to look at Colton. In that nanosecond there was a Kitty-squeal. Sophie forgot Colton, who was now imitating her like an out-of-control flamingo. Tod had the note and was continuing down the aisle, head back, balancing it on his Whoville nose. Which was why he didn't notice Mrs. Y. holding her hands over her head, about to explode. When she yelled, "Class! QUIET!" he jerked his head up and the note fell into Mrs. Y.'s oncoming path. Sophie gasped, and she could hear Fiona doing the same. Kitty was whining like a cocker spaniel.

Mrs. Y. stopped right in front of Tod — and stepped on the little triangle.

"Now!" she said. "Everyone take your seat — immediately!"

There was a mass-scurry as if an anthill had just been destroyed. The only person who had been sitting the whole time was Maggie. But she'd seen it all, Sophie knew, because she, like the rest of the Corn Flakes, was staring at Mrs. Y.'s left loafer with horror in her eyes.

"I'm no longer going to yell to be heard in this classroom!" Mrs. Y. — well — yelled. "Everyone start Microsoft Word and do not speak a single syllable while you're doing it."

Fiona turned to Sophie with her lips already in mid-whisper.

"Not that kind of micro-soft word, Fiona," Mrs. Y. said.

Colton let out a laugh like the kind on TV commercials. "You're really funny, Mrs. Y."

"Yeah, I'm a real crack-up. Now get to work."

The whole class lowered their faces behind their monitors except for the Corn Flakes, who peeked out from the sides to watch Mrs. Y.'s left loafer. The teacher turned to march down the aisle, and the note went with her. It was stuck to the bottom of her shoe.

"We're doomed," Fiona mouthed to Sophie.

Sophie couldn't even mouth back, "Oh, we so are."

After that, it was hard to type and keep track of Mrs. Y.'s constantly moving heel at the same time. The Corn Flakes automatically took turns, and they weren't the only ones.

When Mrs. Y. passed Colton, he pretended to be picking up his pencil — who used a pencil in computer class? — and tried to grab the note. To Sophie's immense relief, he missed. Eddie looked like he was going to shoot a rubber band at it, until Tod hit him over the head with his mouse. Sophie couldn't figure out how Mrs. Y. didn't see that. No wonder the class was a zoo most of the time.

Sophie and the other Corn Flakes were all still watching the progress of the note and the loafer when Maggie tapped Mrs. Y. on the arm.

"You have something stuck on the bottom of your shoe," she said.

Sophie's fingers froze on the keyboard.

"Oh," Mrs. Y. said. She reached down and pulled the note off. "Thanks."

Fiona looked Sophie full in the face and mouthed, "It's OVER."

Sophie closed her eyes, but before she could even beam up Captain Stella Stratos she heard Fiona let out the sigh of the century. When Sophie looked around, Mrs. Y. was tossing their little triangle into the trash can.

Nearby, there was a thud. Eddie Wornom had fallen off his chair.

WHAT HAPPENED? Sophie typed on her screen.

HE WAS LEANING OUT TO WATCH HER AND HE FELL, Fiona wrote back. KLUTZ.

What is so interesting about one of our notes? Sophie thought. *Do I have a sign on my back that says, "Drive Sophie crazy"?*

Sophie looked around to see how the Fruit Loops were reacting. Tod was typing away with a too-innocent look on his face. Colton was looking at somebody and shrugging his shoulders. He was all but saying, *What do you want from me?*

That somebody was Julia.

When the bell finally rang for lunch, Sophie stepped out into the hall to meet the rest of the Corn Flakes.

"That was so close!" Kitty said. Her face was pale to the tip of her nose as she looked at Maggie. "I thought we'd had it when you told her!"

Fiona, too, was looking at Maggie. Although Sophie knew it pained her to do it, Fiona said, "That was pretty smart, Nimbus. Good call."

"I try," Maggie said. As always, her face didn't have an expression.

"So what did the note say?" asked Fiona.

But Sophie put up an elfin hand. "Wait a minute," she said. "Why are we even doing this note thing? Why don't we just talk about it at lunch?"

Kitty giggled. "Because, silly, Maggie — "

"Maggie wants to help, don't you, Mags?" Sophie said.

"How does this solve anything?" Fiona muttered to Sophie as they headed for the cafeteria behind Kitty and Maggie.

"I think Maggie's gonna tell us that herself," Sophie said. "I want to hear her idea about a stakeout."

Fiona twisted her lips. "I do, too. Just when I was starting to really despise her, I have to agree with her."

Sophie linked her arm through Fiona's. This was more like it.

After they all put their lunches in the center of the table, Sophie said to Maggie, "So tell us your idea."

Fiona picked up a half of Sophie's PB&J. "This looks good. We never get this at our house."

Sophie flipped her braids over her shoulders. "All right, Nimbus. Please speak."

"I think we should have somebody in the space station all the time, keeping watch," Maggie said.

"All the time?" Kitty said. "Like, sleep up there?"

"No. All the time from 2:30 in the afternoon until 6:00 and all day on the weekend."

"All four of us at once?" Fiona said.

"No. We take two-hour shifts, two of us at a time."

"Who goes with who?" Kitty said. She clearly had a fearful eye on Maggie.

Sophie looked at Fiona. She hadn't challenged Maggie's idea so far, which meant she actually thought it might work. But her nostrils, Sophie saw, were in the first stages of flaring.

"How should we choose partners?" Sophie said to her.

"I know," Kitty said. "We put our names on pieces of paper and whoever's name we pick is our partner."

They all looked at Kitty in surprise. After all, she usually wasn't the one coming up with the ideas.

"That's what my mom does with me and my sisters when we go anyplace. Everybody has to have a buddy."

Sophie nodded. That made sense. There were six girls in Kitty's family. They would all get sick of one another if they didn't switch off now and then.

"I'll write my and Kitty's and Maggie's names, and then Soph, you pick one." Fiona was already selecting a gel pen from the complete collection in her bag. "Whoever you pick is your partner, and then the other two go together."

"Roger," Sophie said quickly. And then she prayed she wouldn't pick Kitty, which would put Fiona and Maggie together. That could mean the end of the space station before the first hour of the stakeout was over.

She fished around in the Tupperware container Kitty's carrot sticks had been in and pulled out a slip of paper. *Nimbus,* Fiona had written.

Sophie tried not to look stunned. Two hours every day alone with Maggie from now until next week when they turned in their project? Maybe there was another way to do this.

But she held up the paper and said, "It's you and I, Nimbus."

Maggie broke into the biggest smile Sophie had ever seen on her face. A pang went straight through Sophie's chest again.

Well God, she thought, *I guess that must be my job.*

She knew the first thing she was going to have to do in the space station that afternoon was keep Maggie from complaining the whole time that she didn't have any records to keep. Maybe now Sophie would be able to give her the idea she'd been trying to tell the Expedition Crew for two days, only either Fiona or Maggie kept cutting her off: Maggie could write down how long it took for the crew to assemble each part of the space station, which would be sometimes longer and sometimes shorter than it had taken the people in space. She hoped Mrs. Utley would just ignore the fact that the *Freedom 4* was lighter then the International Space Station, like by about a million pounds.

Hey, Sophie thought. *I really am doing my job.*

She just hoped God would do his.

Meanwhile, Maggie wrote up the schedule and had a copy for each of them by sixth period. Even Fiona had to admit it looked very scientific, although she did say to Sophie, "Since I live there, I could come up with you two and hang out."

Sophie got a sudden image of Fiona rolling her eyes at Maggie for two hours, until her eyeballs disappeared completely into her head. It wasn't pretty.

"No, Jupiter," Captain Stella Stratos said. "I know your loyalty to *Freedom 4* goes very deep, but I want you to be fresh for your own shift. You can't properly do surveillance if you're overtired."

"What?" Maggie said.

Sophie sighed. "It means we'll be just fine on our own," she said.

Maybe she could work on Maggie's imagination a little bit up in that tree house and she wouldn't be so bossy and Fiona would stop wishing she would disappear. One thing was for sure — this beat worrying about the Fruit Loops. Besides, if the Corn Flakes could get along and be strong, even the Fruit Loops couldn't drive them nuts.

By the time Sophie got the camera from Boppa that afternoon — because he was keeping it there for her so Mama didn't have to deliver it every day — and got up to the tree house, Maggie was already copying the information Fiona had given her onto one side of a page in a notebook. Sophie watched her while she munched on the Rice Krispies treats Kateesha had transported up to them.

She's really kind of pretty, Sophie thought, *in a scientific kind of way.*

Captain Stella Stratos sat back and watched the businesslike Nimbus work. She is so important to our crew, she thought. We wouldn't be able to achieve our goal without her. Captain Stella Stratos leaned closer to her loyal crew-woman to get a better view of her work. If you would only smile now and then, Stella wanted to say to her.

"Take some joy in saving the planet," Sophie said.

"We're not saving the planet," Maggie said. "We're doing a science project." She edged away from Sophie. "And how come you're practically in my lap?"

Sophie blinked. She was sitting so close to Maggie, they were barely taking up a whole place on the bench. She scooted back.

Maggie put her pencil down and blinked back at Sophie.

"What?" Sophie said. She was getting bristles under her collar. Fiona must feel like this times ten when she was around Maggie.

"We're just trying to keep somebody from tearing this thing apart," Maggie said. "You don't really think we're saving the planet, do you?"

Sophie shrugged.

"Well you don't, do you? This is a little puny science project. The universe goes out for millions of miles."

"Okay, no," Sophie said. She could hear her voice squeaking. "But it seems more real when you pretend."

"But it isn't real."

"But it seems like it."

"So?"

"So — it's fun."

Maggie picked the pencil back up and examined its point. "It's not fun for me," she said.

"Then why — " Sophie bit at her tongue. No, it wouldn't be the Corn Flake thing to ask Maggie why in the world she wanted to hang out with them then. Fiona, she knew, would have asked it in a heartbeat. "Why isn't it fun?" Sophie said.

To her surprise, Maggie's dark face was suddenly fringed in red, and she looked up at the wings and down at the space lockers and out at the robot arm — everywhere but at Sophie. "Because I'm not any good at it," she said finally.

Sophie didn't say anything. After all, Maggie was right about that. She'd just always thought Maggie wasn't even aware that she acted like their robotic arm in every scene they'd ever done for a film.

"Maybe you just haven't practiced enough lately," Sophie said. "How old were you when you stopped playing pretend?"

"I never started," Maggie said.

"Nuh-uh! Everybody plays pretend when they're little." Sophie grinned. "My parents get upset because I didn't ever grow out of it."

Maggie's face got smushy, like she was forgetting to do something with it that she always did to hold it in place. She said, "I wish — "

And then she stopped, and her face went tight and smooth again and she said, "I'm just not a pretending kind of person. My mother says life isn't a fairy tale. She says we all have to grow up sometime."

"Oh," Sophie said. "My mama never says that. She — "

And then it was Sophie's turn to stop. Maybe that was what was happening with Mama. She didn't believe in fairy tales anymore. Or playing. Or even laughing. Maybe Mama had grown up.

Sophie felt a wave of sadness that nearly knocked her sideways. Most of it seemed to land right on her chest.

"All right, Nimbus, back to work," said Captain Stella Stratos. She tried to make her voice crisp, like the people on the Discovery

Channel. "I must continue to document our progress on film. Look scientific, would you?"

Maggie blinked at her and went back to copying. Captain Stella Stratos zoomed in for a close-up. The eyes that had never imagined herself as a unicorn or a princess or a world-famous astronaut went back and forth across the page like the blinking cursor on a computer screen.

I'm so sorry for her, thought Captain Stella. She has no place to go when she's afraid.

Then the captain sighed and closed her eyes and guided the space capsule through a whole shower of flying rocks.

"Don't be afraid, Nimbus!" she cried.

"I'm not," said Maggie.

But somehow Sophie knew she was.

Sophie decided that for the next two days when she was up in the tree house

10

with Maggie, she was going to be Captain Stella Stratos the whole time. Then maybe Maggie would have to start using her imagination more.

The first day, Sophie tried being Captain Stella by herself the whole two hours. Maggie just logged in her information and stared at Sophie every few minutes — as if she were watching an elephant fly.

The second day, Friday, when they had the just-before-dark shift, Sophie peered through the aluminum-foil window and called out, "Meteor alert! Meteor alert!"

Maggie calmly told her that those were not meteors, they were pinecones being pelted at them from below by Izzy and Rory. Seconds later Kateesha appeared and whisked the whole meteor shower into time-out.

Next, as Sophie handed Maggie the granola bars Kateesha transported up to them in the basket, she said, "These are our dried space rations for the day."

Maggie said, "Those were five dollars for a box of fifty at Sam's Club." Then she added, "My mom makes her own."

"She does?" Sophie said. "My mama does, too. Well, she used to — "

It was too sad to go there. Sophie picked up her camera.

"Be Nimbus," she said. "I need some footage of you walking around the space station, hanging on to things so you don't float away."

"I'm not gonna float away."

"Just PRETEND!" Sophie took a deep breath. "We're going to use it in the project," she said. "I need it for GATE points."

Maggie gave that a few seconds' thought, and then she stood up and moved woodenly around the space station, now and then putting a limp hand on an old doorknob turned into a gauge or a lever constructed from a toothbrush handle.

She looks like she's counting heads, Sophie thought. Fiona's eyes would be rolling right up into her brain by now.

"Is that enough?" Maggie said.

"Sure," Sophie said. Just as she was about to push the Off button, Maggie looked down at her feet.

"I can do this one thing," she said. "It's sort of like outer space."

"Do it," Sophie said.

Maggie put one foot behind her and rolled the toes back, and then did the same thing with the other foot, so that suddenly she looked like she didn't have any bones.

"What's that?" Sophie said. She zoomed the lens so she could get the full effect. Maggie was oozing backward, but it seemed as if neither foot ever left the ground.

"Moonwalk," Maggie said. "My mom taught me. We do it in the kitchen all the time."

"Show me how!" Sophie said. She set the camera on top of her locker box and hurried over to stand beside Maggie.

Maggie broke the steps down into slow ones so Sophie could imitate her. It took a couple of toe stubbings to get the hang of it, but within a few seconds they were both gliding around the space station like two astronauts strolling across the moon.

"Look at us!" Sophie said. "We're amazing."

"We could do it faster," Maggie said.

She sped up the steps, legs sliding like she was walking on glass. Sophie tried it and landed square on her buns, feet sprawled out in both directions.

"You fell," Maggie said.

"I did!"

"You can't fall on the moon. There's no gravity."

Sophie's eyes widened. Was this Maggie, *pretending*?

If she wasn't, she was close enough. Being as fluid as she could with a splinter stuck in the seat of her sweatpants, Sophie got up and tried it again. Maggie watched her for a minute, and then her face slowly broke into a grin.

"What?" Sophie said. "What's funny?"

"You. You look like you're a windup toy. Y'know, like you get in a Happy Meal."

"No, I do not!" Sophie said. A giggle bubbled out with the words.

But Maggie nodded. "Yeah. You do." And then she actually laughed. It was a deep sound, and it made Sophie think of chocolate. She had to laugh with her.

"Uh-oh," Maggie said. She pointed a finger at Sophie's camera. "You left it on."

"My battery!" Sophie said. "My father is gonna have a fit."

She picked up the camera and looked in the viewfinder.

"Did you get us?" Maggie said.

Sophie nodded and moved the camera over so Maggie could watch with her. There they were, moonwalking all over the space station, complete with Maggie giving instructions and Sophie dropping on her behind.

Maggie let loose with her rich laugh again, and her shoulders shook so hard, she jerked Sophie's arm and almost sent the camera orbiting into outer space. Then suddenly she stopped.

"Hey," she said. "Am I always that bossy? Like I am on this film?"

Sophie gave her hair a chew. "You know how to do a lot of stuff," she said slowly.

"But I'm bossy," Maggie said. "Don't let my mom see that movie. She'll say I was being President of the World again." Maggie ducked her head, sending the splashy hair down to meet over her nose. "She hates when I do that."

"You and your mom have fun, huh?" Sophie said. "Moonwalking in the kitchen and stuff."

Maggie looked up, and she smiled a very soft smile. "She's like my best friend."

Later, when she was chewing a pencil over her math homework at home, Sophie went back to the picture in her mind of Maggie and her mother dancing in their kitchen, having fun. Every time she thought about it, she felt a sadness flicker through her. It wasn't sad that they had fun together. It was that Maggie's mother was her best friend. That Maggie didn't have one her own age at school.

I remember what that felt like when I first moved here, Sophie thought. *Everybody had a friend but me, until Fiona came.*

But who wanted to be Maggie's best friend? She had said herself she was bossy.

But she could also moonwalk. And she had a chocolate laugh. And she was way smart.

Three reasons why I like her, Sophie thought.

Fiona spent the night with Sophie Friday night. They sat in the middle of Sophie's room with some mini-pizzas from the microwave and the lights off and the covers draped over the headboard to make a tent where they could shine their flashlight. With Lacie and her friend Valerie playing Beyonce on the stereo in Lacie's room and Zeke out in the hall pretending he was Spider-Man and trying to climb up Sophie's door, they had to seclude themselves if they were going to get any best-friend stuff done at all.

"So, Soph—is it awful?" Fiona said.

"Is what awful?"

"Being up in the space station with Nimbus?"

Sophie carefully licked some tomato sauce off her fingers. She knew Fiona wanted her to say it was absolutely heinous—

"It isn't awful," she said.

"But doesn't she boss you around?"

"Sometimes."

"How 'bout all the time?" Fiona peeled a piece of pepperoni off her pizza. "Once this project is over, I think we should just—"

"She taught me how to moonwalk," Sophie said.

Fiona stopped, pepperoni on her lips. "You mean that dance thing?"

"Yeah. It's so cool. I'll show you—"

"I've seen it." Fiona's gray eyes were looking stormy.

"I thought you said you agreed with her about the stakeout idea," Sophie said.

"A lot of good it's doing. Since she's the one we're staking out, you don't think she's going to break something else while we're up there, do you?"

Sophie put down her half-eaten piece of pizza.

"What?" Fiona said.

"I don't really think Maggie's the one who broke our robot arm."

"Oh — so now you're her best friend," Fiona said.

"No!" Sophie said. "You're my best friend."

Fiona slanted her eyes down toward the pizza, but Sophie could tell she wasn't seeing the cheese. "Am I your only best friend?" she said.

"You can only have one!" Sophie said. "Du-uh!"

"Yeah," Fiona said. "Well, sometimes people forget that. I've had it happen." Then she shrugged and held back her head and let a string of cheese drop into her mouth. "Okay — so let's talk about our film. You know all the kids are going to be totally astounded by it."

Sophie nodded, but her mind was twirling around other things.

She's scared I'll like Maggie more than her.

Should I stop getting to like Maggie so Fiona won't get all jealous?

What if I do like Maggie, and Fiona stops being my friend?

Sophie looked at Fiona, who was opening their purple book. Her eyes were shimmering again, the way they always got when the two of them were planning something astounding. She was the made-especially-for-Sophie-LaCroix best friend.

But thinking about Maggie made her squirm. Maggie, who didn't have a special bud. Maggie, who was up to three reasons for being liked. Maggie, who was probably giving everything she had.

The next morning when she and Fiona were brushing their teeth together — with matching toothbrushes — Sophie made a silent decision.

Today the whole time we're up in the Freedom 4, *I'm going to find out more reasons to like Maggie. When I get up to ten — then Fiona will understand.*

When they climbed into Daddy's truck for him to take them to Fiona's, Zeke was already in his car seat in the crew cab.

"Z-Man's going with you," Daddy said as Sophie slid in beside him and let Fiona have the front seat. "He's going to hang out with Izzy and the Ror-meister while you're working."

"Where are you going?" Sophie said.

She thought she saw the crinkles around Daddy's eyes get deeper.

"Your mother and I are going on a date."

"But you're married," Fiona said.

"You don't think a husband and a wife can go on a date?"

Sophie thought about that. Basically, adults could do anything they wanted, so why not? Besides, this sounded good. Mama and Daddy going to a movie and holding hands in there and eating out of the same popcorn. People didn't go on dates if they were about to ... No, this had to be a very good thing.

"I'll watch Zeke and I'll even take care of him tonight if you guys want to go on a really long date," Sophie said.

Daddy broke into a grin. "Okay, who are you and what have you done with my kid?"

To her own surprise, Sophie got a tight feeling in her throat, like she was going to cry.

It's all I have to give, she thought. *It's like MY loaves and fishes. Daddy, don't laugh at me.*

The minute they got to Fiona's, Zeke leaped out of his car seat and crawled across Sophie before Daddy could get the door open. He took off to join Rory and Izzy, with Fiona on his heels to ward off a puppy pile of three kids in puffy coats and with runny noses. It was definitely the coldest day they'd had the whole winter. Icy breath was puffing out of everyone's mouths.

"You sure you want to go up in that tree house today?" Daddy said to Sophie. "You're going to freeze your nose off." He reached down and caught her nose gently between the knuckles of two fingers. "It's too cute for you to lose." Then he looked at her closely.

"Are you crying, Soph?" he said.

"I think so," she said. She blinked hard. "I just wanted to help."

Daddy put his hand on her cheek. It almost swallowed it up. "You do help," he said. "Just by being you."

Then he coughed and reached back into the truck. "If you're determined to go up there," he said, "you're going to need this." He pulled out a thermos. "Hot chocolate. They drink it in space. I have it on the best authority."

It made Sophie smile a damp smile.

Maggie was, of course, already up in the space station when Sophie climbed the ladder, trying to write down more stuff with her gloves on. She had a bright yellow scarf pulled over her nose and mouth.

Sophie pulled out the blanket she had stuffed into her backpack and wrapped up in it. Then she produced the thermos and dug in her locker for two cups.

"Maybe we should watch the station from inside the house," Sophie said as she poured. "It's way cold up here."

"I will not abandon the *Freedom 4* in her time of need," Maggie said.

Sophie almost poured the rest of the hot chocolate right over her hand. She sucked on the glove finger where it dripped some and tried not to stare at Maggie.

Reason Number Four: Maggie is loyal.

Maggie joined her and took a cup with steam curling up from it. As Sophie was blowing on hers, Maggie said, "I'm not trying to be the boss of you, but I think you did something you weren't supposed to."

"For real?" Sophie said.

"You left your camera up here yesterday."

Sophie spit the sip she'd just taken back into the cup.

"I put it in your locker when I got up here this morning. Are you gonna get in trouble?"

Maggie's eyebrows were scrunched up, like she was really worried.

"Only if it's broken," Sophie said. She squeezed her eyes shut. "I can't look. You check it."

"I already did. It works okay." Sophie opened her eyes to see Maggie nodding very seriously. "You're lucky it didn't rain last night."

"Please," Sophie said. "That would be so heinous."

She was about to take another sip of her hot chocolate when there was a scream so loud from the direction of Huntsville, they both abandoned their cups and got to the railing.

"They shouldn't be doing that," Maggie said, voice as calm and heavy as ever.

Sophie's was not. "No kidding!" she squeaked.

Rory was hauling a little red wagon across the lawn, bouncing it through the now-empty flower beds and nearly turning it over when he got to a walkway. Which was not good, since Izzy was in the wagon, holding on to Zeke. Sophie realized she had to hold on to him because he couldn't hold on for himself. He was wrapped up in enough rope to tie all three of them up. He was the one doing the screaming.

"Somebody's gonna get hurt," Maggie yelled down at them.

If Rory heard that, he ignored her. He careened the wagon around a curve in the walkway on two wheels, just missing Kateesha, who was coming at him with both arms out. She had to step off the walk to avoid being plowed over, but that didn't stop her from reaching into her coat pocket and pulling out something that she put in her mouth. A high-pitched whistle made Sophie put her hands over her ears. And it definitely brought Rory to a sneaker-screeching halt.

In minutes Kateesha had Zeke untied and she was dragging both Izzy and Rory toward the house by the backs of their collars.

"Captain Stella!" she called over her shoulder. "Could you take Zeke on board for a few minutes?"

"I'm not allowed to," Sophie called back to her.

But Kateesha was too busy telling Izzy and Rory how long their time-outs were going to be to hear her. Sophie looked down at her little brother, who was looking up at her with his eyes twice the size they usually were. He looked smaller than ever from outer space.

I can't just let him stand there and freeze to death, Sophie thought. *Mama will understand.*

Sophie tried not to think that maybe the new grown-up Mama wouldn't, and helped Maggie get the still-hollering Zeke up the ladder. While Maggie closed the hatch cover, Sophie poured enough hot chocolate in him to make him stop howling. Then he looked around, and his eyes started to shine.

"This is COOL!" he said.

"He shouldn't touch anything," Maggie said.

Zeke looked at Sophie. "Is she the boss of me?"

"She's the president of the whole world," Sophie said.

"Nuh-uh!" Zeke said. And then he peered at Maggie from under his knit cap and said, "Are you?"

"No," Maggie said. "I just act like I am."

Reason Number Five: Maggie didn't lie about herself.

Maggie smiled at Sophie like they had a secret. Sophie made that Reason Number Six.

"What's over here?" Zeke said. Instead of pointing, he got up to stomp across the hatch cover toward the robot arm.

And then suddenly, he was down again. There was a silence, the kind that always came when Zeke fell and he was deciding whether to cry or not. He evidently thought he needed to because the wail he sent up went right through Sophie.

The minute she got to him, she saw why. The hatch cover had split right down the middle, and Zeke's leg was wedged between the two halves. Sophie watched in horror as blood soaked into his jeans.

Sophie thought the floor was breaking open under her, too. And

then she realized she was just sinking down to her knees, staring at the blood.

"Go get help!" she said. "He's hurt bad! He's bleeding all over the place!"

Maggie got down beside her and bent over Zeke. "Stop crying," she said to him.

Her voice was so calm it made Sophie want to scream louder.

"You have to answer some questions," Maggie said.

To Sophie's utter amazement, Zeke choked back his tears to a lower level. "Can you move your leg?"

"Nuh-uh. It's stuck."

Zeke puckered up again.

"Okay — how about the part that's hanging down?"

Sophie realized for the first time that his leg had gone all the way through and it was dangling from the knee down. Zeke swung it a little and then started yowling again. There was no quieting him this time.

"You go get help," Maggie said to Sophie. "I'm gonna cover him up with a blanket and stuff."

"I can't! He's on the hatch cover!"

Zeke's shrieks went way up into the atmosphere, and Maggie looked hard at Sophie and then at Zeke. Sophie bit her lip.

"It's okay, Z-Man," Sophie said to him. "I'll get help some other way."

She went to the railing and shouted for Kateesha, for Boppa, for anybody. It wasn't hard, since she wanted to scream anyway.

But her shivery shouts seemed to disappear with the puffs of frosty breath that blew from her mouth. Then Fiona burst out onto the deck, dragging Boppa behind her. Boppa ducked back into the house and came out with a cell phone in his hand. Fiona was already standing at the bottom of the ladder by then, staring up at Zeke's dangling leg. Sophie had never seen her best friend look so white and wide-eyed.

"He's bleeding!" Sophie called to her.

"Boppa's coming!"

Their two voices tangled up into one high-pitched knot. Maggie's voice was the only calm one.

"He's not going anywhere," she said.

Sophie looked over to see that Maggie had Zeke bundled up and lying down with his other leg up. Zeke was still crying, but he wasn't making a lot of noise. He was watching Maggie's face as she talked to him, and he was nodding. Sophie figured Maggie was telling him he would be fine — or else.

Boppa's bushy eyebrows looked jet black against his skin as he took in the board situation. He was pretty white-faced himself.

"Okay," he called up to Maggie and Sophie. "I'm going to get up there and pry the parts of the board apart. You two are going to take Zeke by the armpits and pull him back, very slowly."

"Very slowly," Sophie said. She could hardly hear her own voice.

"Just get him so his leg is clear of the hole and don't move him any other way."

Maggie looked at Sophie. "That's in case it's broken," she whispered.

"Okay, ready?" Boppa said.

Sophie half crawled over to Zeke and got behind him on one side. Maggie took the other, and Sophie could see her holding her breath.

"One, two, three," Boppa called. "Now!"

Sophie could hear the boards splitting apart, and she and Maggie gave Zeke one gentle tug. Sophie covered her eyes and waited.

"His leg's still in one piece," Maggie said. "All in one piece is good."

Boppa was there like Spider-Man himself, with Fiona crawling in after him. He knitted his eyebrows over Zeke's leg and nodded. Sophie decided Boppa nodding was good, too.

"It's not as bad as it looks," he said. "I'm calling Fiona's mother."

Sophie and Fiona clung to each other like baby monkeys while they waited for Fiona's doctor mom to get there. Sophie watched as Maggie helped Boppa get Zeke in a position where he fell into a soft whimper instead of the screams that were shaking the pinecones out of the trees.

I don't know what number reason I'm on, Sophie thought. *I just know I like Maggie enough for anything.*

When Dr. Bunting got there, she said Zeke needed to go to the emergency room. Boppa got on the phone and called Mama and Daddy to tell them to meet them at the hospital.

That was when it hit Sophie like a blast of frozen air. Mama had told her never to take Zeke up in the tree house. She was going to be so upset — so disappointed — so mad — that this could be it. The final thing. Just when she'd started to be Mama again.

Even Captain Stella Stratos can't fix this one, Sophie thought. *Because it's all my fault.*

By the time Sophie, Boppa, and Dr. Bunting got Zeke to the hospital, Mama and Daddy were already there. Sophie felt like she could almost see through Mama's pale face.

Things went by in a blur. From what Sophie could tell, Zeke was being put in a room with curtains, Dr. Bunting was telling Mama he would barely feel a thing, and Daddy was leading Sophie down the hall for interrogation.

He squatted down in front of her so that their heads were the same level. She was afraid to look into his eyes, so she fixed hers on the third button down on his shirt.

"What happened, Soph?" he said.

"I don't know," she said to the button. "I told you I'd watch him, and I was. I was protecting him from Rory and Izzy — and I'm not dreaming, he really was in trouble — "

"Soph," Daddy said. "Take it easy. I'm running out of breath."

She looked at his face. His eyes were shiny, not angry.

"Just tell me what happened. One word at a time, okay?"

But Sophie couldn't seem to slow herself down. "Mama told me not to let him go up there, but I had to — Kateesha told me to and

I couldn't just let him stand down there and be all frozen—but Mama's going to be so upset with me she'll really leave us now!"

Sophie sucked in some breath, and her eyes went back to Daddy's button. "Are they going to have to amputate?"

Suddenly Daddy's big arms were around her, pressing her glasses right next to the button. "No, Soph," he said. "He'll get a couple of stitches and a Tootsie Roll Pop and he'll be driving us all nuts again within the hour."

Sophie started to cry, big old sobs that soaked Daddy's shirt. He just let her bawl until the tears dried up. Then he held her out in front of him with both arms.

"Now listen to me," he said. "Mama isn't going anywhere. I don't know where you got that idea, but she's our mama and she's staying right here."

All Sophie could do was stare. It was all too much to store in her brain right now.

"We'll talk about that some more later," Daddy said. "But right now, I want you to try to focus with me, okay?"

Sophie nodded.

Daddy got his face very close to hers. "Do you have any idea who cut that board?"

"Cut it?" Sophie said. She could feel her eyes bulging. "You mean, like, on purpose?"

"Boppa says he's sure someone cut it with a saw so when somebody put weight on it, it would break."

Sophie went cold. Daddy watched her face.

"One thing I can count on from you, Soph," he said in a soft voice, "is that you're always honest."

Sophie riveted her eyes to the button again, but Daddy tilted her chin up. She had to look at him.

"I don't know who it was," she said. "Fiona will say she does, but I don't think so because I have five — no — six reasons why I like that person and I know she wouldn't do it."

"And that person is?"

"It wasn't me," a voice thudded from the doorway.

Sophie whirled around, slapping Daddy in the face with her braids. Maggie was there, and her mom was right behind her. Senora LaQuita looked like she wanted to smother somebody.

"Fiona already told her dad she thought I did it," Maggie said. "Only I didn't. The only time I've been up there is when I was with somebody."

Senora LaQuita took Maggie's shoulders and pulled her back against her. "My daughter doesn't lie," she said.

"Mine doesn't either," Daddy said, "so I guess that puts Maggie in the clear."

But Maggie pointed a finger at Sophie, and for once her voice wasn't heavy and strong. It sounded like it was going to break.

"You do too lie," she said. "You told Fiona you thought I did it, but you told your father you didn't, so you're lying to somebody."

Sophie could feel her mouth dropping open. "I didn't — "

"I don't lie!"

"Neither do I!"

"Okay, whoa," Daddy said, hands up. "That's something you two are going to have to figure out on your own." He glanced up at Senora LaQuita. "Unless you want to take it on."

The senora gave him an are-you-kidding look.

"Nobody here thinks you cut the board, Maggie," he said, "so the important thing is to find out who did." He looked back and forth from Sophie to Maggie. "Any other ideas?"

But Sophie's mind couldn't even turn in that direction. She was still watching Maggie, who was staring hard at the floor. There wasn't a chocolate laugh within miles.

Maggie, I didn't tell Fiona that! Sophie wanted to cry out.

And then another thought seized her. Why would Fiona say she had?

With the deepest pang in her chest yet, Sophie knew Maggie was telling the truth. It was her beloved Fiona who was lying.

"Why don't we all just think about it?" Daddy said. "We'll sort this out after we get the Z-Boy home." He put his big hand on Sophie's shoulder and looked at Maggie. "You two okay? No bumps and bruises?"

Sophie shook her head. Maggie still wouldn't look up.

"I want to thank you, Miss Maggie," Daddy said. "I under-stand you really kept your cool up there in the tree house. Good job."

Maggie finally lifted her head a little then. But she didn't smile. She didn't look at Sophie. She just thudded out, "You're welcome."

Sophie felt a thud of her own. It was her heart dropping.

Zeke got his stitches and his sucker and fell asleep in the truck on the way home. Sophie sat in the backseat with him, her mind reel-ing. Actually, it was Dr. Stella's mind that was reeling.

The Freedom 4 *has been sabotaged right under our noses, she thought. And now the crew is divided. How is this to be solved? How am I going to talk to Astronaut Jupiter in a scientific way —*

Sophie came back to herself with a supersonic jolt. Once again, Dr. Stella couldn't make it okay with her way of looking at things. There was nothing scientific about this at all. This was about a best friend. A best friend who lied.

This time Sophie closed her eyes and pictured Jesus — whose eyes were sad.

What do I do? she said to him in her mind.

He didn't answer. He never did in words. She tried to remem-ber what Dr. Peter said. Ask the questions, go to the Bible, and then wait for the answers. But what could the loaves and fishes possibly have to do with this?

When Sophie got home and was passing through the kitchen, Lacie pulled her head out of the refrigerator and told her that Fiona had called and wanted Sophie to call back. Sophie squeezed her eyes shut.

Just this once, couldn't you give me the answer right NOW? she said to Jesus.

"What's the matter? Do you have a stomachache?" Lacie said.

"Sort of," Sophie said.

To her surprise, Lacie was nodding. "This has been a rough day. I'd be surprised if you didn't puke. I feel like I'm going to."

And then she turned to the door where Daddy was carrying in the still-conked-out Zeke. Sophie watched her, chin dropped, for a few seconds.

Did that just happen? she thought. *Was Lacie just actually nice to me?*

But there was no time to think about that much, because the doorbell rang. When Sophie opened the door, Fiona and Boppa were standing there. Sophie's heart took another thud.

"We brought your camera back," Boppa said. His caterpillar eyebrows were sunken over his eyes.

"Why?" Sophie said. "Aren't we still going to use it?"

Fiona let out a loud breath through her nose. The nostrils were at an all-time flare.

"Hey, Soph," Daddy said behind her. "You going to make everybody stand out in the cold?"

He ushered Boppa in and did the usual guy handshake thing. Sophie could only look at Fiona as they stood there by the door. She was fuming like Sophie had never seen her do before. Before Sophie could go back to Jesus one more time and beg for some words, Fiona grabbed her arm and dragged her to a spot by one of Mama's tall plants.

"You are not going to believe this," she said. "It's so heinous I can't even tell you."

"I need to tell YOU—" Sophie started to say.

But Fiona forged ahead. "They're having the tree house taken down."

Sophie could feel her face freeze. "The *Freedom 4*?" she said.

"Yes! My parents said it was too dangerous and even though Zeke didn't get hurt that bad they don't want anybody else getting injured so they're having somebody take the whole thing down Monday."

The nose breaths were coming hard and fast now.

"But what about the space station?" Sophie said.

"They're saving that. They said we could set it up in the garage."

"But the film isn't finished—"

"I know! I told them this was so unjust and that Maggie is the one who should be punished, not us. But they—"

Sophie stopped listening to her. Words were orbiting in her mind, but they weren't confusing anymore. She shook her head.

"What?" Fiona said.

"Maggie didn't do it, Fiona."

There was a short silence, and then Fiona said, "Of course she did."

"She said she didn't, and I believe her."

With an impatient hand, Fiona brushed back the leaves that were tickling the side of her face. "You believe her? Just because she said so." The eyes rolled. "Sometimes you're just too trusting, Soph."

"You told Maggie that I didn't believe her."

"I thought you didn't."

"I told you I didn't think she broke the robot arm."

Fiona craned her neck forward. "But I thought after you said we were still best friends, you would think what I thought. We've always thought the same thing."

Slowly, Sophie shook her head. Fiona took a step back.

"Then I guess we're not best friends after all," Fiona said.

"WHAT?"

"As soon as we're done with the space station," she said, "I think we should just not be best friends."

Sophie couldn't breathe. She could barely get out her next words.

"Not be best friends?" she said.

"Uh-oh."

It was a soft voice, just on the other side of the tree. Sophie peeked through the leaves at Mama.

"Trouble, my loves?" she said.

"No," Fiona said.

"Yes," Sophie said. She looked at Fiona through a blur of tears. "You just said we weren't going to be best friends anymore."

"Wow," Mama said. "This sounds like something that needs to be discussed over some of that gingerbread I made this morning. Come on, follow me."

For a minute, Sophie forgot that Fiona was about to end the best friendship in the entire galaxy. Mama was talking. Mama was baking things. Was Daddy right? Was she really there to stay?

Still, Sophie felt a stab as Fiona sat herself on one of the snack-bar stools and looked the other way. It didn't look like her best friend was there to stay.

"Lemon sauce?" Mama said, ladle poised over a bowl.

Fiona shook her head. Sophie didn't even answer. Mama put the spoon down and folded her arms on the countertop facing them.

"The best thing to do is to talk this out," she said. "Obviously there's been a misunderstanding, and believe me, the only way out is to go through."

There was something sort of I-know-about-these-things in Mama's voice that made Sophie listen to her very carefully. Fiona still didn't turn her head, but she nodded a little.

"All right," Mama said. "Could you use a moderator?"

"What's that?" Sophie asked.

"It's somebody who talks for people when they aren't speaking to each other," Fiona said.

"You can be that," Sophie said.

Mama smiled her elfin smile. "Okay. Now, I understand that you, Fiona, think Maggie cut the board that Zeke fell through. And you, Sophie, don't think she did it."

"And Fiona told Maggie that I did think so," Sophie said.

"And she believes her instead of me so I can't be her best friend anymore."

"Do best friends have to agree on everything?"

Fiona looked at Mama as if she'd just arrived from another planet's space station. "Yes. How else can they be best friends?"

Mama cocked her head, curls brushing against the side of her face. Sophie was getting a full feeling in her throat. THIS was her mama.

"Do your mom and dad agree on everything?" she said to Fiona.

"Uh, how 'bout no?" Fiona said. "They had an argument this morning about where the new hot tub is going to go."

"Okay—does that mean they aren't best friends?"

Fiona gave her another you're-from-outer-space look. "Are parents supposed to be each other's best friends?"

"Oh, most definitely," Mama said. "And one of the things that makes them best friends is that they know how to disagree. And that's what you two have to figure out. How to keep liking each other even though you don't think alike every second."

There was a silence. *I'm already doing that,* Sophie thought.

"I just get petrified," Fiona said. Her voice was thick.

"Petrified of what?"

"Of Sophie not wanting to be my friend. I never had one before, not like her. I was so scared of her liking Maggie better than me, I watched them in the tree house through binoculars this morning. That's how I knew Zeke got hurt."

Tears were trickling down Fiona's golden cheeks. Sophie started to cry, too.

"Sophie," Mama said. "Do you have any plans to stop being Fiona's friend?"

"No!" Sophie said.

"What would it take for you to stop being friends with Fiona?"

"I would never do that!" Sophie said. "Not unless she did something really heinous—like hurt somebody—"

"Speaking of which."

Sophie and Mama turned to see Daddy standing in the doorway. His face was solemn, like he had bad news. Sophie was pretty sure she'd had enough bad news to last her whole life.

"Speaking of hurting somebody?" Mama said.

Daddy nodded. "I think you should all come in here and see this."

They followed him into the family room, Fiona trailing along behind as if she didn't want to have to talk to Sophie. Sophie was trailing her heart behind her.

Daddy had the camera turned on, and it took a second for Sophie to realize he was showing what they'd done on their film so far. Not much was happening at the moment. There was only a view of the empty *Freedom 4*.

Daddy cocked one eyebrow at Sophie. "We'll talk later about why you left your camera up in the tree house running for an hour last night after you and Maggie left. But I think you're going to be glad you did it."

The film continued, still showing the floor of the station, murky in the darkness. And then there was a darker shadow, cast by the hatch cover coming up. And then a head. And a set of ears that stuck out from somebody's head.

"Is that Colton Messik?" Fiona said.

Sophie nodded and watched another figure struggle through the hole, breathing like a tractor. "And that's Eddie Wornom. I'd know that backside anywhere."

"Okay," Daddy said, "now who's this kid?"

Another figure hauled itself up through the opening, plunking something on the floor ahead of him. It was a short guy who moved like he was in charge. It was Tod Ravelli, grabbing what she could now see was a saw and hissing something to Eddie's bulky form. The hatch cover came down over the opening.

And then a tearing sound suddenly ripped from the film, as Tod's elbow appeared over and over.

"Mercy," Mama said. "He's cutting that board."

"And we've got it on film." Daddy turned to look at Fiona. "There's your scoundrel."

Fiona stared at the top of the coffee table, and Sophie could tell she was blinking back tears again.

Sophie sat up tall. "We can handle them, Daddy. We'll — "

But Daddy put up a hand. "Soph, this is way too serious. This isn't some schoolboy prank. It was done deliberately, and you need to let adults handle it."

Sophie sank back against the cushions. It was okay. Even Captain Stella Stratos would let the big commander do his job.

Boppa got on the phone with Tod's parents and there was a lot of, "Yes, I'm sure. Of course, I'm certain. I would never make an accusation like this without being absolutely — Yes, I'll bring the film over."

Boppa and Daddy left, and after Mama made sure Sophie and Fiona weren't crying and scared, she went upstairs to check on Zeke. That left Sophie and Fiona sitting in the family room on opposite ends of the couch, acting like they didn't know each other. Sophie did feel like crying then.

And it wasn't because the Fruit Loops had something so bad against them that they had actually tried to hurt them. It was because Fiona was so far away.

I want to fix it — I hate this! But I don't have any words. Jesus isn't giving me the words!

Fiona was running her toes back and forth across the coffee table and hugging a sofa pillow and looking miserable.

I have to say SOMETHING, Sophie thought. And she opened her mouth and let out the only words she had.

"You were wrong about Maggie, but anybody could make a mistake. I did."

Fiona shook her head, still sliding her toes on the coffee table. "You're never wrong. You're just way better than I am."

"But I was wrong. I thought Nimbus was too bossy at first, too." Sophie scooted closer to Fiona. "She's not so bad, Jupiter. She's smart. She does the moonwalk. She has a laugh like chocolate and she's loyal and she knows first aid and she knows she's bossy."

She could see Fiona swallowing.

"But she doesn't know way-cool words and she doesn't have the best imagination in the universe and she doesn't know how to be somebody's friend. But I'm teaching her that." It was Sophie's turn to swallow hard. "And then she'll find her own best friend."

Fiona looked at Sophie with very round eyes. "Then you're not gonna trade me for her?" she said.

"Best friends don't DO stuff like that!" Sophie said. "I guess I need to be teaching you, too."

Fiona hugged the pillow tighter to her, and Sophie thought about Dr. Peter's window seat. She felt a little like Dr. Peter must feel sometimes. She even wrinkled her glasses up her nose.

"I'm sorry I lied to Maggie about you not believing her," Fiona said.

"Okay," Sophie said.

Fiona looked at her with agony in her eyes. "Are you sure you don't hate me?"

"I'm sure," Sophie said solemnly.

Fiona looked down at her toes. "I bet Maggie will hate me forever."

"You don't want her to?" Sophie said.

"No! But what do I do?"

"How 'bout we call her?"

"You call her for me," Fiona said.

Before Sophie even started shaking her head, Fiona was rolling her eyes. "Okay, okay, I'll call her — only you have to be right there with me."

"Hello!" Sophie said. "Of course!"

It actually was Sophie who got Maggie on the phone, because she knew she would probably hang up if she heard Fiona's voice first. She was pretty surprised she didn't do it when she heard Sophie's. As it was, Maggie's words were thudding harder than usual.

"I'm mad at you," she said to Sophie.

"I didn't tell Fiona I thought you cut the board," Sophie said. "And she wants to tell you that herself."

"Wants" might have been too strong a word. Fiona looked like she would rather have hit herself in the head with the receiver than talk into it.

But Sophie was proud of her. She took the phone and took a breath and spilled out an apology in that one big burst of air. And then she deflated like a bicycle tire as she listened to Maggie talk. Sophie got next to Fiona so they could share the earpiece.

"Okay — I guess I forgive you," Maggie said. "Only I don't see why you had to lie."

"Because I thought you were going to take Sophie away from me."

"Take her where?" Maggie said.

Fiona rolled her eyes at Sophie. "You know, become her best friend instead of me."

"Oh," Maggie said. "No, I never have best friends."

"There isn't any reason why we can't all be best friends," Sophie said as she crowded her mouth next to Fiona's. "You and me and Kitty."

Fiona looked like she suddenly had the stomach flu, but Sophie held up a wait-a-minute hand. "Fiona's my BEST best friend, but you and Kitty can be my other best friends and we can be yours and Kitty's."

Maggie didn't say anything for so long, Sophie wasn't sure she was still there. When she finally answered, she said, "Okay. I'll bring the costumes over tomorrow."

Fiona collapsed against the couch.

"We have to have a meeting tomorrow anyway," Sophie said. "We'll tell you what's happening with the *Freedom 4* then."

When she hung up, Fiona was laughing. And laughing. And laughing.

"What?" Sophie said.

"I don't know," she said. "I just feel like laughing."

Sophie kind of did, too.

Boppa and Daddy came back before an hour was up, and once again they and Mama and Fiona and Sophie gathered in the family room. Mama brought out the gingerbread and sauce, but nobody ate it.

"Tod confessed," Daddy told them. "Under duress."

"What does that mean?" Sophie said.

"He didn't want to do it," Fiona said. "I could have told you that."

"What's going to happen to him?" Sophie said.

"I don't know, but his father assured me he'll take care of it and it will never happen again."

"I want to believe that," Boppa said. Even his eyebrows looked sad. "But to be on the safe side, Fiona, I want you to avoid those boys at all costs."

"Uh, hello," Fiona said. "I wouldn't go near them if you paid me."

"Me, neither," Sophie said. It felt good to be agreeing with Fiona again.

"He doesn't take all the blame, though," Boppa said. The lines in his face looked like they were about to laugh.

"So he told on Eddie and Colton, huh?" Fiona said. "Like we hadn't already seen them on the movie."

"It isn't them he was blaming," Boppa said. "It's your old pals — what do you call them? Cheerios?"

"The Corn Pops?" Fiona said. "No way!"

But Sophie was bobbing her head up and down. "Yes, way! I saw Julia looking at them when they were trying to get the note off Mrs. Y.'s shoe the other day. You know, THAT look?"

Fiona nodded. "Oh, yeah. I know."

Daddy blinked at both of them. "What just went on?"

"It's a best friend thing," Mama said. "Known only to girls."

"Oh," Daddy said. "That would explain it. So we told Tod if he wanted to turn them in for putting them up to it, that was their choice, but he was the one holding the saw."

"Does that mean we can't turn them in?" Fiona said.

Daddy shook his head. "All you have is what Tod said."

"Too bad," Fiona said. "I'd like to see them go down again."

And then she looked at Sophie. Sophie was shaking her head.

"Or not," Fiona said.

Mama sat down on the arm of the sofa and put her hand on Sophie's shoulder. "I am really concerned about all this bullying. From now on, I want you to tell us every time anything like this even gets started. This has gotten way out of hand."

"Mama's right," Daddy said.

Sophie nodded until her head hurt. The only thing better than she and Fiona agreeing was Mama and Daddy agreeing. It was the best thought of the day.

Later, when everyone was gone, Mama came into Sophie's room.

"Whatcha thinking about, Dream Girl?" she said. She sat down on Sophie's bed next to her. Sophie scooted closer.

"I was thinking about loaves and fishes," Sophie said.

"Okay," Mama said. She didn't sound the least bit surprised. "And why were you thinking about loaves and fishes?"

"I don't know. I was trying to figure out what to do about Fiona and I asked Jesus to help me and I even thought about the loaves and fishes story because Dr. Peter said it would help but it wasn't helping ..." She stopped for a breath. "And then it worked out anyway."

"What did you do to get it to work out?" Mama said. She crossed her legs in front of her and began to unbraid Sophie's hair with her tiny Mama hands.

"I just said what was in my head." Sophie rolled her eyes. "It really wasn't eloquent at all. And it wasn't scientific, which is what I'm into now."

"I've been sort of out of the loop on that. We'll have to get caught up." Mama ran her fingers through Sophie's loosened braid and gently shook out the crimped-up hair. "I think I know how the loaves and fishes story worked for you — because it's worked the same for me."

Sophie turned her eyes to Mama without moving her head, since Mama was now working on the other braid. "Did Dr. Peter give you that assignment, too?" she said.

"No," Mama said. "You just made me think of it. I know I haven't been myself lately and I'm sorry for that. I know it's been hard for you."

"I didn't fall down in my grades, though!" Sophie said. "I'm still in GATE — and we'll make the space station amazing, even in the garage — "

Mama stopped unbraiding and closed her eyes for a tiny second. "I know, and I'm proud of you. But you had nothing to do with my being unhappy."

"Then why were you?"

"For a lot of reasons that I've talked to Daddy and Dr. Peter about," Mama said. "Daddy and I have worked out our tangles, and God and I have worked out mine."

She leaned across to the bedside table and picked up Sophie's brush. Sophie wriggled herself around and felt it run smoothly down the back of her hair.

"But when everything was in knots," Mama said, "I had trouble doing the things I needed to do."

"I know about that," Sophie said.

"Yes, you do. And I bet you know that when that happens, you can only give what you have, and God will fill in the rest until you really start listening to him again." Mama gave her soft laugh. "The answers are always there, of course."

Sophie let her head fall back as Mama went on brushing.

"Mama?" she said.

"What, Dream Girl?" Mama said.

"Does that mean I don't have to fix everything? You know, like make everything okay for everybody?"

Mama stopped brushing, and Sophie could feel Mama's forehead pressing against the back of her hair.

"That's exactly what it means," Mama said. "All we have to do is love and act like we love. That's what Jesus does, right?"

Sophie closed her eyes right there and imagined herself in the hungry crowd. Only it wasn't on a hillside. It was in a school, and people were fighting and throwing things. Kind of like in Mrs. Y.'s class. She could picture Jesus standing up in the middle of all those kids and—not yelling—saying, "All right. Who has something that can quiet down all this racket and get everyone getting along?"

Sophie looked down at her hands. She wasn't holding anything. But she knew there was something she could give. Something she would always have with her.

I know there's a reason to like every person here, she told Jesus. *I've got a bajillion for Dr. Peter and a bunch for Fiona and I'm getting a big list for Maggie, too. I'm even starting to like Lacie.* She took a whisper breath. *Anyway, that's all I have. If people could just look at the good reasons . . . That's all I have.*

Mama slid her arms around Sophie. "I don't know where you are right now, my Dream Girl," she said. "But wherever it is, I think it's a very good place to be."

It was a good place, Sophie decided when Mama was gone. She snuggled into the pillows. Now if she could only think of a reason to like the Corn Pops. That was a dream she'd save for tomorrow.

Glossary

advantageous (AD-van-tage-us) doing something that helps you out

aeronautics (AIR-oh-nah-ticks) the science of flying airplanes

amputate (AM-pew-tate) to remove someone's leg or an arm

calculations (kal-kyu-LA-shuns) addition, subtraction, multiplication, division, or a mix of all

cease and desist (seese and de-SIST) a command made by someone in charge that means to stop being unfair

clandestine (clan-DEHSS-tin) secret in an almost sneaky way

degradation (de-gre-DAY-shun) when something really bad happens to you and you feel bad about yourself

duress (der-RESS) someone who does something only when forced to do it

endure (in-DUR) to deal with or accept that something is happening

heinous (HAY-nuhss) shockingly mean, beyond rude, or like wicked in a bad way

imbeciles (IM-buh-sulls) complete and total idiots

imperious (im-Pir-E-us) acting all snotty and stuck-up, like a spoiled empress

intergalactic (in-ter-ga-LAC-tick) a place in space that is somewhere between earth and really, really outer space

microgravity (my-crow-GRAV-i-tEE) when gravity becomes really weak and everything just floats around

moderator (mod-er-A-ter) someone who acts as a messenger when people are in huge fights

nanosecond (NAH-no-sec-und) one-billionth of a second, or the time it takes for everything to go wrong

ozone (O-zone) the hazy layer around the earth that keeps us from frying up and getting really sunburned

pact (packt) a promise to do something, no matter what

sabotage (sa-bo-tahge) to cheat by purposely wrecking something someone else did so you can win

scathingly (sKAY-thing-lee) to insult someone in a totally rude way, meaning to hurt their feelings

scintillating (Sin-till-ATE-ing) something that is really fun, interesting, and exciting

stratosphere (Stra-tuh-sfear) the highest point of the earth's atmosphere, or the last level of air on earth

Sophie LaCroix couldn't believe what she had just heard.

1

There was no way Miss Blythe had just announced that the sixth-grade class was going to get to do a Performance Showcase — on the stage — on a Saturday night — in front of a REAL AUDIENCE. And that the top three performing groups would each get a prize.

In Sophie's world, dreams like THAT just didn't come true every day. Sophie's best friend, Fiona, grabbed her hand and squeezed it until Sophie's fingers looked like red lipsticks.

"Do you think she'll let us pick our own groups?" Kitty whispered on the other side of Sophie. Her blue-jay-blue eyes were nearly bulging, the way they always did when she was nervous. Which was a lot.

"She would be nonsensical not to," Fiona whispered back. "We're the Corn Flakes."

"So?" That came from their other friend, Maggie, whose voice thudded across the table they shared. "Teachers don't care about that."

Sophie looked at Miss Blythe, who had her back to them, writing dates and times and requirements on the board with flowing chalk. She was their arts teacher, and Sophie had often thought she couldn't be anything else.

Miss Blythe was tall and wore long skirts and bracelets that flounced with bright-colored charms. She swayed like a new tree when she walked, the strands of her waist-length blonde hair streaming down her back as if they were rays of sunlight. With her long fingers constantly punctuating her sentences in the air, Sophie had a hard time imagining her as a lawyer or a greeter down at Wal-Mart. And Sophie could imagine just about anything.

Is Miss Blythe the type to let friends—best friends who can't bear to be separated—work together? Sophie thought. *Or would she subject her students to pure torture at the hands of girls like the Corn Pops?* They'd only had arts class for about a month. It was hard to say.

"I can't work with Julia and them!" Kitty was whining. She did that a lot, too. "She and B.J. and Anne-Stuart and Willoughby—they would be so mean to me!"

"Yeah, they would torture you," Maggie said in her usual flat, factual voice. "Any of us."

Sophie could tell by the way Kitty was whimpering that none of that was making her feel any better. It wasn't doing much for Sophie, either, for that matter. She shook her acorn-colored hair off her shoulders and adjusted her glasses as she leaned into the table. The rest of the Corn Flakes leaned in with her.

"We just have to pray really hard," she said. "We have to squeeze our eyes shut and whisper to God in our heads."

"That'll look weird," Maggie said. Sophie saw that she was on the point of rolling her very dark eyes. Maggie was Cuban, so everything on her was dark except her extra-white teeth.

"Corn Flakes are weird," Fiona told her. "That's what makes us unique. Close your eyes."

They all did, clutching each other's hands under the table. Just before she shut hers, Sophie saw the Corn Pops clinging to each other, too, but she was pretty sure they weren't praying.

In fact, Sophie wondered if the Corn Pops EVER prayed. What they did do, as far as Sophie could tell, was think they were better than everybody else because they had more money than rock stars and could get their way no matter what. "No matter what" included cheating, lying, gossiping, and teasing people about anything they thought was too weird.

And since the Corn Pops considered everything the Corn Flakes did way too weird, Sophie and Maggie and Kitty and Fiona were their favorite targets.

At least we used to be, Sophie thought now. *Until they got in so much trouble for doing bad stuff and blaming it on us.*

It was a little bit of a comfort that the Corn Pops wouldn't dare do anything else to the Corn Flakes, at least not anything they could possibly get caught at. But Sophie knew the Pops had ways of getting away with things that could escape even the really smart teachers. She sure hoped Miss Blythe knew a Pop from a Flake and wouldn't try to mix them together.

It's pretty easy to see the differences, Sophie thought.

The Corn Pops only wanted to be popular — which was why they were Pops — and they would do anything to stay the boss of everybody else in the sixth grade at Great Marsh Elementary, which was where the corn part came from. Sometimes they were so corny in the stuff they did.

Sophie squinted her eyes open a little so she could peek at her fellow Flakes. Fiona, with her rich-brown bob that fell over one of her gray eyes. Maggie, so serious and stocky and practical. And Kitty, with her curly ponytail and her little nose that looked like it was made of china.

Corn Flakes are corny, too; that's what everyone says, Sophie thought, *just because we like to make up stories and make films out of them, and we don't care what anybody else thinks about that.*

Once, back when Kitty was still a Pop, the CPs had said Sophie and Fiona were a couple of "flakes." It was so perfect it had to be their name. After that, the girls who were all into sports were the Wheaties and most of the boys were Fruit Loops. The best part was that all the group names were a secret among the Corn Flakes.

"If everyone is awake, I'll finish explaining the project," Miss Blythe said.

Sophie's brown eyes sprang open, even though she hadn't actually gotten to praying at all. She pulled her elf of a body up as tall as she could in her chair. It wouldn't be good to be caught daydreaming, or Daddy would take her video camera away from her, and Corn Flake Productions would be no more. That was the deal with her father — stay out of trouble and make nothing less than a B in school and she could keep the camera. Mess up, and it was all history.

"I want at least four people to a group," Miss Blythe said. "And I feel very good about letting you choose your own — "

The rest was drowned out by shrieks that bounced off the walls and back again. Even as Sophie was hugging Fiona and hoping Kitty wasn't going to spill off her chair into a puddle of relief, she saw that the Corn Pops were every bit as excited. B.J. — the pudgy-faced one with the swingy blonde hair — was whistling through her teeth. Willoughby, of course, was letting out one of her poodle laughs that could set a person's fillings on edge, and Anne-Stuart was blowing her nose. Anne-Stuart had sinus issues. She was always blowing her nose.

Above it all was the Corn Pop Queen Bee, Julia Cummings, tossing her thick, curly auburn hair back from her face and looking as if she had expected nothing else. After all, she always got what she wanted.

Even as Sophie watched her, Julia turned to meet her eyes. Julia's went into slits, but she wore a smile that looked as if she'd selected it from a rack of grins and stuck it onto her face. Sophie had learned that every one of Julia's smiles had a message to send. This one clearly said, *Thank heaven I didn't get stuck with any of you.*

Sophie smiled back — a real smile. People always told her that her smile was wispy, like a wood fairy's. Sophie didn't know about that — she just knew that right now, it wiped Julia's own grin right off her mouth and replaced it with another message, etched into a sneer:

Don't even think about getting a prize, Sophie LaCroix, because we are so going to win.

"All right — let's settle down," Miss Blythe called out above the din. "Artists are disciplined people — remember that."

She perched on the high stool at the front of the room and began to make periods and commas in the air with her long fingers as she talked.

"Each group must discover an idea for a performance that is to last no more than ten minutes at the very most."

One of the Wheaties, a softball-playing girl named Harley, poked her arm into the air. "What kinda stuff can we do?" she said. Her group all had their foreheads in twists, Sophie noticed.

"Anything the audience might enjoy," Miss Blythe said. Her eyes took on a dreamy look. "You can sing, dance, do gymnastics, present a poem — "

That got a couple of snickers from some of the Fruit Loops, but Miss Blythe ignored them.

"Think about what gifts and talents the members of your group have and put them together into something fabulous. And remember . . ." She arched an eyebrow at the class. "You will be graded not only on the performance itself, but also on how organized you are and how well you are able to work together."

Sophie sighed happily. Maggie would be in charge of organization. Maggie, herself, and Fiona would do the thinking. And Kitty would do whatever they wanted her to because she always did.

"We are so going to have the best one," Fiona whispered to them.

"I want you to meet with your groups now," Miss Blythe said, curving a comma with her pinkie finger, "and go to work on coming up with an idea. I need to see it in writing by one week from today. That's next Thursday. If you have nothing by then, I will assign a poem for your group to present."

"She'll have ours way before next Thursday," Maggie said.

As soon as Miss Blythe punched out the final period with a deep purple fingernail, Maggie got out the Corn Flakes' purple Treasure Book and the special color-of-the-day gel pen, a shade of pale peach. Fiona got her finger around the strand of hair that hung over her eye and twirled it. Sophie recognized that as her creative thinking pose. Sophie's was to tuck her way-skinny legs up under her and gaze at the ceiling.

It was Kitty, however, who spoke first. "Good thing we already know what our talent is. What can we make a film of?"

"Film?"

They all looked up at Miss Blythe, who had stopped beside their table with a swish of her lavender skirt.

"That's what we do," Fiona told her. "We write scripts and make films out of them. They're always educational. We do our research and we have costumes and — "

"I'm impressed," Miss Blythe said. "But you can't make a film for the Sixth Grade Showcase. This has to be a live performance."

Then she looked at the Corn Flakes as if they obviously didn't know what art really was and swept off to visit the Wheaties.

Kitty's voice immediately spiraled up into a whine. "But what do we do if we can't make a film?"

"Not fair," Maggie said.

"I'm gonna go talk to her," Fiona said.

But Sophie held up a hand. "We'll think of something else," she said. "I get in trouble when I argue with teachers."

Fiona plucked at her little bunch of a mouth with her fingers. "Let's go around the table and everybody say what their talent is — besides making films."

For a long moment, nobody said anything. Finally Fiona snapped her fingers.

"I used to take ballet," she said.

"When?" Maggie said.

"When I was five. Only my parents had to take me out because the teacher didn't like me. I kept correcting the way she was pronouncing the positions. She was saying everything wrong."

Maggie had the peach pen poised over the blank page. "So Fiona can dance, but I can't."

"Me neither," Sophie said.

Kitty shook her head.

"Next," Maggie said. "I can make costumes, period."

"And you're the best at it," Sophie said. "Whatever we decide to do, you get to make them for us."

Maggie jotted that down and then looked at Kitty.

"Me?" Kitty said. "I can play the piano. Except the only song I know is 'You Ain't Nothin' But a Hound Dog.' My grandma taught me it. She says it's a classic."

"You know my talent," Sophie said. "I imagine things."

"So what are you imagining right now, Soph?" Fiona said.

"Oh, no," Kitty whispered suddenly.

Sophie followed with her eyes to where Kitty was pointing. All the Corn Pops were squealing up to Miss Blythe's desk, and Anne-Stuart was waving around a piece of paper, which she floated down in front of Miss B.

"They couldn't have their idea written up already," Maggie said. She glanced at the wall clock. "It's impossible."

Fiona narrowed her eyes into little points. "They probably cheated."

"Class!" Miss Blythe said. She shot her index finger up into an exclamation point. "Julia's group has already come up with a marvelous idea! They are going to perform a dance with costumes. Doesn't that sound fabulous?"

"Fabulous," said some Fruit Loop in a bored voice.

"Okay, Flakes," Fiona hissed between her teeth. "Everybody has to come up with at least one idea by tomorrow morning — even if it's lame."

Maggie wrote that down, too.

"I know your idea won't just be average brilliant," Fiona said to Sophie. "Yours will be scathingly brilliant."

"Oh, by the way — "

That was Anne-Stuart's voice, coming out of her always-stuffy nose. "We are going to need one more dancer. If you are interested in being in our spectacular production, see me and we will set up an audition for you."

Sophie pulled her Corn Flakes in around her with a spread of her arms.

"I'm glad none of us can dance," she said. "Because we will always stick together, right?"

They all agreed that they would. Always.

faiThGirLz!

Faithgirlz!™–Inner Beauty, Outward Faith

Sophie's World (Book 1)
Written by Nancy Rue
Softcover 0-310-70756-0

Sophie's Secret (Book 2)
Written by Nancy Rue
Softcover 0-310-70757-9

Sophie's Irish Showdown (Book 4)
Written by Nancy Rue
Softcover 0-310-70759-5

Sophie's First Dance? (Book 5)
Written by Nancy Rue
Softcover 0-310-70760-9

Sophie's Stormy Summer (Book 6)
Written by Nancy Rue
Softcover 0-310-70761-7

Sophie Breaks the Code (Book 7)
Written by Nancy Rue
Softcover 0-310-71022-7

Available now at your local bookstore!

zonderkidz

faiThGirLz!

Faithgirlz!™—Inner Beauty, Outward Faith

Sophie Tracks a Thief (Book 8)
Written by Nancy Rue
Softcover 0-310-71023-5

Sophie Flakes Out (Book 9)
Written by Nancy Rue
Softcover 0-310-71024-3

Sophie Loves Jimmy (Book 10)
Written by Nancy Rue
Softcover 0-310-71025-1

Sophie Loses the Lead (Book 11)
Written by Nancy Rue
Softcover 0-310-71026-X

Sophie's Encore (Book 12)
Written by Nancy Rue
Softcover 0-310-71027-8

Available now or coming soon to your local bookstore!
Visit **faithgirlz.com**—it's the place for girls ages 8–12!!

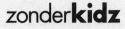

faiThGirLz!™

Faithgirlz!™–Inner Beauty, Outward Faith

Now Available

Coming May 06!

No Boys Allowed:
Devotions for Girls
Written by Kristi Holl
Softcover 0-310-70718-8

Girlz Rock:
Devotions for You
Written by Kristi Holl
Softcover 0-310-70899-0

Chick Chat:
More Devotions for Girls
Written by Kristi Holl
Softcover 0-310-71143-6

Available now or coming soon to your local bookstore!

zonder**kidz**

faiThGirLz!

Faithgirlz!™–Inner Beauty, Outward Faith

Grace Notes
> Written by Dandi Daley Mackall
> ISBN: 0-310-71093-6

Love, Annie
> Written by Dandi Daley Mackall
> ISBN: 0-310-71094-4

Just Jazz
> Written by Dandi Daley Mackall
> ISBN: 0-310-71095-2

Storm Rising
> Written by Dandi Daley Mackall
> ISBN: 0-310-71096-0

Available soon at your local bookstore!
Visit **faithgirlz.com**—it's the place for girls ages 8–12!!

faiThGirLz!™

Faithgirlz!™—Inner Beauty, Outward Faith

With TNIV text and Faithgirlz! sparkle, this Bible goes right to the heart of a girl's world and has a unique landscape format perfect for sharing!

TNIV Faithgirlz!™ Best Friends Bible
Hardcover: 0-310-71002-2

Available
August 2006

TNIV Faithgirlz!™ Best Friends Bible
Faux Fur: 0-310-71004-9

Available soon at your local bookstore!

We want to hear from you. Please send your comments
about this book to us in care of zreview@zondervan.com. Thank you.

Grand Rapids, MI 49530
www.zonderkidz.com